Pangyrus

For information about permission to reproduce selections from this book,
please write to Permissions at info@pangyrus.com

The text of this book is set in Palatino
with display text set in Crimson and Baskerville
Composition by Yahya Chaudhry and Abraar Chaudhry
Cover design by Douglas Woodhouse

Editor: Greg Harris
Managing Editor: Sarah Colwill-Brown
Associate Managing Editor: Robin Beaudoin
Assistant Managing Editor: Ahna Wayne Aposhian
Fiction Editor: Anne Bernays
Poetry Editor: Cheryl Clark Vermeulen
Nonfiction Editors: Marie Danziger, Jess McCann
Comics Editor: Dan Mazur
Contributing Editors: Kalpana Jain,
Carmen Nobel
Editorial Assistants: Yahya Chaudhry, Graeme Harcourt
Graphic & Web Designers: Esther Weeks, Erika Rich
Copy Editors: Chris Hartman,
Ahna Wayne Aposhian, Rachel Zwiebel
Business Manager: Lakeisha Landrum
Logo Design: Ted Ollier

Pangyrus
79 JFK Street, L103
Cambridge, MA 02138
pangyrus.com

Contents

Note from the Editor   9

the dark, it quivers by Claudia Cortese   13
Crows with Sun by Kevin McLellan   14
One of Those Calls by Jared Yates Sexton   15
Allegheny Cemetery Day in Winter by David Blair   20
The War at Home: Baltimore by Sebastian Johnson   22
Nous Sommes Paris by Joelle Thomas   26
Greetings from Paradise by Janine Oshiro   31
What Lucy Feels Like by Claudia Cortese   33
That the mind isn't guided by the punished shade
          by Tony Mancus   35
Manger by Suzanne Matson   36
The Synthetic Option by Whit Taylor   41
Toast by Gus Rancatore & Corky White   49
NOW IT IS JOY THAT IS PROHIBITED — THE THING THAT
          ESCAPES ALL ECONOMIES by Kara Candito   56
Congo: the Story of One Family's Endurance by Lisa Shannon   58
Lucky Jews by Erica Lehrer   63
Switch or Axe by Michael Walsh   71
Oliver Sacks: A Hero's Journey by Harvey Blume   73
Reporter's Notebook: Inside the Brothels of Mumbai
          by Shanoor Seervai   89
I Want to Tell You Something by Susan Volchok   93
The Truth of Low-Hanging Clouds by Jonathan Weinert   98
The Pervert by Dwight Livingstone Curtis   100
Aphorisms for a Lonely Planet by Lance Larsen   127
Expedition Notes by Carrie Bennett   129
Astronomy by Mitchell Krochmalnik Grabois   132
Esperantists by Dan Mazur   135
I Blog Therefore I am by Judy Kugel   147

Boys of Summer by Molly Howes — 155

Return to Fort Scott: An American Hometown in Black and
White by Paul A. Tamburello Jr. — 163

Fire Fetched Down by Jennifer Marie Donahue — 167

Megafauna by Erica Anzalone — 169

Your Beautiful Robot Face! by Dustin Luke Nelson — 171

Contributors — *172*

About Pangyrus & Index — *179*

Pangyrus

Note from the Editor

One of our goals at Pangyrus has been to improve the publishing experience for authors. I'd spent years, and seen friends and students spend years, ginning up courage to send out stories, hearing nothing for months, only to finally receive a rejection that said nothing about what had gone wrong.

Now, I thought, I'll be on the other side of the desk as editor. I'll fix all the things I hated.

There are real limits, though, to editorial time and attention. An email came in recently from an author whom we'd made wait, and whose story we'd been forced to reject despite some promising qualities.

I sat looking at it. I was in China at the time, taking advantage of jetlag and the time difference to put in a 36-hour day of teaching and editing technical documents—working to stay solvent, since editing literary magazines is a labor of love ('love' here meaning exactly what it does in tennis).

Maybe it was exhaustion, or that my window let in the red glare of the hotel's enormous Cold War era sign, "The Friendship Palace," promoting a long since dead Soviet-Chinese Communist cooperation. But it occurred to me that the real problem for those who would reinvent the wheel is not, as the cliché would have it, that they are doing something useless; rather, it's that they are doing something hard. Any truck lumbering down the road is a collection of dozens of specialized variations on wheels, from spinning axles and discs to fans and belts and ball bearings and gears. Decades of refinements have gone into each.

So, too, between the founding of The Atlantic Monthly in 1857 in our hometown of Boston, and today's 5,812 literary publishers on the subscription-based writer's network Duotrope, a tremendous amount of talent and invention has been devoted to serving writers and readers. In all that time, two truths have prevailed: authors wait too long, and good work gets too often rejected. In every published correspondence between authors and their editors, there are urgent pleas for attention. Somewhere on my shelves I have copies of Knopf's internal communications about Sylvia Plath, Stephen King, Vladimir Nabokov, and other authors—all of whom got turned away.

To think that we at Pangyrus were going to solve that out of the gate—no. On the other side of the editor's desk, there is the power to encourage success—and the humbling reality of having to disappoint.

Luckily, that's not the whole picture. We're still at an early stage of our efforts at Pangyrus, and yet we've published 150+ authors—many of them first-time authors. We've brought together a team of talented editors and designers, and built a readership. And as to submissions, we've put together a new initiative to bypass the worst of the slush pile experience: we ask you, our readers, to nominate writers who ought to be in our journal. Let us know what you love about an under-exposed author's work, and we'll send him or her an invitation to run stories by us. It's not a promise to publish, of course—but a promise that we'll read each submission with close attention. And it's a message to the writer from you: you believed, and you cared enough to act.

Details are on our website.

It's been a real pleasure working with our talented Pangyrus team to usher this second volume of work into the world. Our dream has been to connect stories and voices from across genres and across the world and, as a result, the reach of this second collection is tremendous. To take just a few far-flung examples from our non-fiction: Sebastian Johnson's "The War at Home: Baltimore" brings a passionate, clear-eyed voice to the racial and policing issues that roiled America this year; it complements Joelle Thomas's reporting, in "Nous Sommes Paris," on issues of global terrorism, and the fight to address climate change. Lisa Shannon's intimate witness of conflict in "Congo: The Story of One Family's Endurance," meets the intimate portraiture of "Fort Scott," reviewed by Paul Tamburello, and the travel reporting of Shanoor Seervai.

And then there's the fiction, that dissolves us into the seething, conflicted bed of a long-time couple in Susan Volchok's "I Want to Tell You Something"; the splintered love, and holiday gone wrong, of Suzanne Matson's "Manger"; and the ordinary, but nearly unmanageable neighborhoods of adolescence in Dwight Livingstone's "The Pervert." New to this edition is the inventive comics journalism shepherded our way by Dan Mazur, our new comics editor. His "Esperantists" and Whit Taylor's "The Synthetic Option" are inventions in storytelling we're proud to publish.

The poetry that begins and ends our collection is no exception. Both Cheryl Clark Vermeulen, who edited most of the work here, and Gregory Lawless, our founding poetry editor, have an eye for verse that brings us into an experience of language that's both intimate and capacious. We start with the quivering darkness of Claudia Cortese's portrait of girlhood submerged, and end contemplating death and love among the robots that carry on the neuroses of us, their creators; in between we range from the white-hot emotion of Michael Walsh's "Switch or Axe" to the cool metaphysics of Dustin Luke Nelson's "The Truth of Low-Hanging Clouds."

Pangyrus owes a tremendous debt of gratitude to our contributors, our writers, our supporters and volunteers, and the goodwill of a community that stretches from Cambridge and Boston to all corners of the world.

A few of our pieces are enjoying a second life, by gracious permission of their publishers. "Nous Sommes Paris" by Joelle Thomas, "The War At Home" by Sebastian Johnson, and "Reporter's Notebook: Inside the Brothels of Mumbai" by Shanoor Seervai, appeared in slightly different form in The Kennedy School Review, with which we have a co-publishing agreement. "Return to Fort Scott" by Paul A. Tamburello, Jr. appeared in The Arts Fuse (www.artsfuse.org). "Congo: The Story of One Family's Endurance" by Lisa Shannon is an excerpt from her wonderful book, Mama Koko and the 100 Gunmen: An Ordinary Family's Extraordinary Tale of Love, Loss, and Survival in the Congo, published by PubliCAffairs in 2015. "One of Those Calls," by Jared Yates Sexton, originally appeared in The Hook and the Haymaker (Split Lip Press, 2016). Both "The Synthetic Option" and "Esperantists" appeared in SubCultures, edited by Whit Taylor and published by Ninth Art Press, 2014.

If the project, like the name, of Pangyrus is conceptual, it's up to our cover designer, Doug Woodhouse, to make it all into something tangible. He finds maps, then plays with the lines, teasing them into the space of thought and feeling. We hope this volume takes you, our readers, on a similar journey.

—Greg Harris

the dark, it quivers

by Claudia Cortese

the dark, it quivers
I loved your skin
lit me through
you see
until we
in between
the bully
the nails
we suffer
and then
cat-lit
the distance
that 90s kitsch

in that corporate way
its glow-in-the-dark frame
dark alleys
we are all body
are no longer body
we suffer
the mannequin
teeth-plucked
till suffering blooms
the alleys turn
laugh-lit knife-lit
of payphone booths
our girlhoods died in

Crows With Sun

by Kevin McLellan

CROWS

a determined
them sometimes
on the branches
of today

you left
remain now as
a question
in dark things

WITH SUN

crowd of
companions
stain the brightness
a year since

you chose to leave
not quite a shadow and
I see you
in white on white

One of Those Calls

by Jared Yates Sexton

WHEN HE GOT good and drunk and the night wore on he liked to get on the phone and call up ex-girlfriends. He had a letter to write that evening though and so he sat down on the porch to write it before retiring to the phone. It was already dark outside at that point. Luckily he'd replaced the bulb in the porch light the week before and all it would take to get some light would be to walk inside and flip the switch. When he went in though he got sidetracked. He had to carry all his empty cans in and that led to getting another beer and that led him to the kitchen where the phone was screwed into the wall.

He looked at the ragged piece of paper on the counter with all the numbers.

By this point most of his ex-girlfriends had learned to just let the phone ring. Some got angry and told him never to call again. Christine was one of the last few who would put up with him and so that was who he called.

Hello, Christine said.

Hi there, he said. It's Chappy.

Chappy, she said like she wasn't sure she knew a Chappy.

How goes it?

Just fine, he said. Aces and kings.

Sure thing, Christine said. You sound drunk.

There's a mighty fine reason for that, he said.

And that is?

Because I'm drunk, he said.

Uh huh, she said.

Hey, he said. You busy, darling?

Nothing I can't finish later, she said. What can I do for you?

Well Christine, he said, I was just sitting down to write a letter and I needed to ask somebody a question. A real serious question.

If this is one of those calls, she said, I can't handle it right now. We didn't work out and that's the end of it. It's been four long years. I can't handle you crying and begging.

Okay, he said.

Okay meaning that's what you called for, or okay, you understand?

Understand, he said. Loud and clear.

Good, she said. Okay. The question.

He said, The question is important. Real important.

Okay, she said.

And I want you to answer. The truth. Nothing but.

Hell, she said. What is it, Chappy?

Well, he said, here it is. Do you think I'm some kind of terrible sonuvabitch?

What? she said.

He said, You know me pretty good, Christine.

Chappy, she said, I told you I couldn't handle one of these phone calls.

No, he said and got another beer. It's not one of those calls. He looked in the refrigerator and opened a drawer and then shut it. It's a question, he said. I need to know.

Where's this coming from?

I don't know, he said, looking at the pen and paper he'd planned on using to write the letter. They were sitting on the kitchen table next to a phonebook he'd left out in the rain. I'm writing a letter, he said, and I want to get it right.

A letter? Christine said. It's not a letter to me, is it? Cause I can't handle that either.

No ma'am, he said. Unless you want a letter.

No Chappy, she said. The last thing I want is a letter.

Okay. Well, I got a letter to write, he said, and I need to know if maybe I'm some kind of sonuvabitch. If maybe I just didn't realize it.

Christine didn't answer at first. The line went so silent he thought maybe she'd hung up. He even said Hello, you still there? and she said she was and was thinking of a way to say something.

Chappy, she said, finally, slowly, I think you're a fine person, a good one sometimes, but you can act like a real sonuvabitch.

He rolled that around in his head and took a drink of his beer and picked the pen off the pad of paper and opened the soggy phonebook. While he thought out what she'd said he ran the tip of the pen across a random page and the page ripped open like a zipper.

That's fair, he said into the phone.

I think you get lost, Christine said. You're a sweetheart most times, and I think you've got a good heart but you get lost. You set your sights on something else, she said and paused. Someone else, she said. And then you turn into a real asshole.

Right then he remembered this one time, back when Christine and him were still together, when they'd lived together, and he'd come home from a fishing trip. She'd been sitting at the same kitchen table that was in his kitchen. She was smoking and drinking a gin and tonic. He told her all about the trip and how he'd been in the boat with his friend and a storm had turned up, an electrical storm, and how lightning kept hitting the water around them.

We almost died, he told her. The real deal. We rowed like madmen to get to the shore. And the waves were crashing down and we kept getting turned around and losing track of where we were going.

She'd looked at him and took a long, stiff drink of her gin and tonic. After she'd swallowed it down she said, You asshole. Just pick a direction next time and go.

Hey, he said to her through the phone, remember when I was caught in the storm in that boat?

Sure I do, she said. I gotta go though, Chappy. Things to do.

Sure thing, he said. Hey, thanks for picking up.

No problem, she said. He heard the clink of what he figured to be ice cubes floating in a sea of McCormick's. And Chappy, she said, I should tell you. Kent proposed last month.

What'd you say? he asked.

Yes, she answered. I said yes.

Hell, he said. You're settling.

Well, she said, whatever. I don't care what you think. You don't have the right to criticize considering you never asked.

Tell you what, he said. I'm gonna catch the next flight out your way and propose.

Oh god, she said. Don't.

No, he said. I'm gonna make you say no to me.

Chappy, she pleaded.

Okay, he said. Just be ready when you hear that doorbell.

Goodnight, she said. And good luck with that letter.

When she hung up he ran upstairs and packed a suitcase and a bag for his toothpaste and deodorant and shampoo. He'd already made up his mind to get on a plane and propose to Christine, but when he got downstairs with his bags he saw the pad of paper and pen sitting on the kitchen table.

He paused. Set the bags down and got another beer out of the fridge.

Outside he sat on his porch again. Already he knew what he wanted to say in the letter, what words and phrases he wanted to use, but he didn't start right yet. He sat there in his chair and drank his beer and listened. For an hour or so it was quiet and it gave him some time to think. But then the night got darker as clouds took form. Lightning flashed in the distance and he thought, maybe, for a second, he heard thunder rolling in from behind.

Allegheny Cemetery Day in Winter

by David Blair

Windows above the doors,
as I remember it, at the Board of Health,
tuberculosis skin test station nearby
built when even waterworks
were pretty in a way, green copper visors
over red brick blackened in time,
and the feeling of file cabinets
full of sputum and vials
of venereal samples,
slices of human lung prepared
for slides, as if the biology
room had mated with raccoons,
or I got that idea from the entry
to the Allegheny Cemetery,
home of the bones
of Steven Foster,
and bones attached
to place names and streets
Wightman and Negley,
and Rankin, where a friend
was the son of a Russian priest,

and the swells' planting
contiguous with roughened up places,
Bloomfield, Friendship, Lawrenceville,
and carved Union cloaks
draped over tombstones,
and the incinerated remains
of the Armory workers
who exploded, and Josh Gibson
with his bat. My own bat,
I dreamed of after walking
there in the cold. It was mad
because I sliced its belly
with a potato peeler
and bonked it with the potato grater
as it flew at me in the kitchen,
making latkes, or maybe gnocchi.
Bat dreams, maybe they are good,
just an early threadbare Pittsburgh
boiled down to abstract streets
with its Scotch-Irish aristocrats
still somehow Presbyterian
with their Gothic fonts
and conspicuous paucities.
The vistas of sunsets and lagoons
were lit up in all the stained glass
mausoleums turned on by sundown,
the irrationality we bring ourselves
or in it comes in with clouds from the lakes.

The next day, we all felt a bit fevered and ill.

The War at Home: Baltimore

by Sebastian Johnson

*Neither slavery nor involuntary servitude – except as a punishment
for crime whereof the party shall have been duly convicted – shall exist within the United States, or any place subject to their jurisdiction.*

– 13th Amendment to the United States Constitution

The war at home is calling your father on his birthday, and finding out he's back in jail. It's the familiar resignation in your
grandmother's voice, the empty pleasantries exchanged, and the
lump in your throat that refuses to melt away.

The war at home is the coat clutched tightly around your shiv-
ering frame, the itch in your eyes from the fine dust accumulating
in their corners, as you sit in a building too hot in the summer and
too cold in the winter. It's the teacher barking orders over too many
students, the ratty textbook and the desk shared with two others.
It's the gnawing hunger in your stomach where breakfast should
be.

The war at home is anxious, darting eyes and apprehensive
paces, straining to see around corners, seeking to cut through air

heavy with menace. It's the muscle memory that threads your steps through city streets, past the corners where trouble lurks. It's the nihilistic violence of the hopper, and the caprice of the cop on his beat.

The war at home is the omnipresent knot of dread, the foreboding sense of impending calamity. It's the trash bags that hold your possessions, awaiting your next eviction. It's the tears that well in your eyes that first night in the homeless shelter, your shame when you return to school the next day in the same clothes. It's the furtive consumption of your free lunch, and the awkward drape of your Salvation Army sweater. It's the darkening of your mind when you come to realize the American Dream will not be your inheritance. It's a lifetime of Top Ramen instead of a brief college diet.

The war at home is a secret wish for blue eyes and the unquenched thirst for acquisition. It is the rearranging of values that manages to uncover some hidden path to material wealth. It's the admonition to be twice as good to get half the loaf – and being content with a quarter. It's working hard, and playing by the rules, even when the rules don't work for you anymore. It's the belt cinched tightly at the waist, the permanently plastered smile, and adopting the Queen's English.

The war at home is the sour taste of small successes. It coats the tongue like the hard memory of last night's binge. It's the intended compliments that serve as epithets: Oreo. Whitest Black Person I Know. Not Like The Others. It's the uneasiness that congeals, double-consciousness that becomes both shield and crutch, the self-hatred turned outward at those who share your hue but refuse to play the same game.

The war at home is your quickening heartbeat when you find yourself behind a white woman on an empty street. It's keeping your hood down, even if your ears are cold. It's the effort to allay an unspoken suspicion. It's whistling Vivaldi as twilight falls to signal that you are "one of the good ones."

The war at home is being jolted out of the New Black Dream. The unambiguous signs of your otherness; the cab driver that speeds past your outstretched arm; the slight edge in the police officer's voice when she cites you for a small violation; the person at the party who asks who it was that invited the black guys. The slow drip of circumstance thatserves as reminder: "Oh that's right, we are just some niggers. I almost forgot."

The war at home is silently waged. It is gaslighting on a societal scale. It's the pervasive skepticism and erasure that greets black experiences. It's plausible deniability and second-guessing. It's the friend who assures you that you're overreacting, the small voice inside that tells you he's right. It's the obsessive reliving of bad memories, the dull drumbeat in the background of your daily interactions. It's the racist society that doesn't see race.

The war at home is terror, fast and slow. It's sweaty palms gripping the steering wheel at 10 and 2, on the side of a road in broad daylight. It's the leaden feeling in your chest as the officer ambles to the driver's side window. It's the banal interaction gone tragically wrong. It's adrenaline making a split-second decision to run or fight. It's six shots in the front or eight shots in the back. It's a broken neck and a crushed voice box. You can't breathe. Fuck your breath.

There are no heroes in this war, only casualties. No medics are called when their bodies fall to the earth. No comfort is offered to the afflicted, and only malice to their widows and orphans. No wall will commemorate their names. When their blood cries for justice from the ground, we counsel patience. We wait for the facts. We lament the misfortune. We imply they deserved it.

It is a war waged unceasingly and unyieldingly. To end it would require a will that our nation does not possess. The war rages interminably, as shattering as the common history we cannot embrace. And yet, in our fervent dreams, in our battle hymns, we affirm the dignity of black life in a time cheapened by black death. We stretch out upon our faith in a future unseen, where the children of men will study war no more.

Nous Sommes Paris

by Joelle Thomas

I love Paris.

Walking through the world's most beautiful streets for the Climate Conference reminded me of why. To me and to so many, Paris represents a romanticized idea of what life should be like; a life that values time spent pursuing the arts, vivacious conversations with friends in picturesque cafes, an afternoon furiously scribbling down the meaning of life after a bout of inspiration during an afternoon stroll. A life that values love and passion, art and culture, and offers an escape from small worries that occupy too much space in our minds. A brief promise that life can be more than what we know. For generations, people from around the world have found solace, inspiration, and answers in its streets.

But those of us who know Paris noticed a city slightly altered. Just the month before, the streets and cafes that make Paris's heart beat were terrorized as seven attackers committed acts of heinous violence that will forever shake the sense of personal security of those who reside within the city's extraordinary walls. Cue a slew of expressions of solidarity, moments of silence, flags at half mast, and days of action. And then the world's monuments and everyone's Facebook walls lit up in bleu, blanc et rouge.

Now, security guards and police interrupt the bustle of the metro, which runs half empty as commuters take to their cars for fear of another attack. The city mourns its losses in many ways, but most remarkably, through a beautiful display of flowers, candles, and quintessentially French cartoons at the historic Place de la Republique—site of the solidarity march of world leaders after the Charlie Hebdo attacks earlier this year. Interspersed between the ribbons and wreaths are poignant messages of resilience, courage, peace, and unity.

Paris goes on. In fact, it goes forward.

In the wake of the attacks, the leaders of the world looked to Paris for answers to one of the toughest problems of our time: how to stop the irreversible damage to our planet from climate change. French Foreign Minister Laurent Fabius did not miss a beat in announcing that the Paris Climate Conference would go on as planned following the terrorist attacks. It was a bold statement to terrorists that they would not disrupt business as usual. And, not a single one of the 120 world leaders slated to attend cancelled their trips.

Why? Because, to those who care about civilization, Paris is personal. An attack on Paris feels like an attack on values that we hold dear. It is more than the senseless killing of 129 innocent people; it feels close to home—it's in our backyard, and if violence can happen there, it can happen anywhere. It was a bid to disrupt the entire fabric of daily life, and our ability to look ahead. To take the horrific violence that has already ravaged Syria, Lebanon, Afghanistan, Iraq, and so many places, and place it in the heart of Europe. To make violence "the new normal" everywhere.

So too, another "new normal" emerges before our eyes, but stealthily, more subtly, over time. The irreversible damage to our planet due to climate change has already started to take its violent toll on ice caps and weather patterns, and we too often stand by quietly, watching as our emissions ravage the stratosphere. No one is immune to the catastrophic consequences of poor air quality, massive forest fires, desertification, and rising sea levels, all of which will cause massive population displacement in our lifetimes if we don't change course now. But only some regions have started to experience the problems, while others, wealthier or more protected from the effects of sea level rise and forest fire and storm, haven't yet felt strong effects. It's not personal. At least, not yet.

In ways, Paris became, with the attacks, an even more appropriate setting for the climate conference. Because to solve both problems, to defang extremist violence and extreme weather, we need to overcome a dangerous "us and them" mentality. In Paris, "they" are the youth, whose names and faces identify them as members of a troubled 'other.' "They" are politically and culturally disenfranchised, and physically kept at the margins of the city. Everywhere, "they" are the marginal, the disempowered of disintegrating countries, or refugee camps. Struggling for a vision of how their lives and sacrifice will have meaning, despairing of ever reaching the inner circle that promises opportunity, respect and dignity, "they" become vulnerable, in these spaces, to radicalism, to the threat and allure of violence in the name of purity. This is the breeding ground of ISIS, and other causes that seem self-evidently insane and mindlessly destructive to "us," who have never felt so disenfranchised and excluded by the system as to want to break it.

And in climate change, "they" are the far-off Pacific islanders who practice their traditions in unfamiliar tongues and lead unfamiliar lifestyles. "They" are vulnerable populations of farmers who await rains that do not come, who ask themselves how they will survive if they cannot make the $2 dollars a day their crops yield under normal conditions. "They" did not cause this damage, but they are the most vulnerable, the most affected by climate change.

And their voices are powerless, with the exception of annual meetings like the climate conference in Paris. The rest of the year, the "us" sit comfortably in air-conditioned homes and fuel-inefficient cars, inflicting a different kind of violence on our planet.

Now, Paris is an opportunity to admit that we will no longer be "us and them," but to empathize with the lands and forests lost and the collective harm we've done. It's an opportunity for a new kind of radicalization—a radical shift in the way we see the world's resources: not for plundering, but for protecting.

The climate conference in Paris is an opportunity to fight bad with good.

It took senseless violence in the streets of the City of Lights to fire us up about the threat of ISIS, to worry about homegrown terrorism, and to ask why we didn't realize that the daily manslaughter in Syria would affect us too. How many cities will sink under water before we realize we should have cared about climate change with the same urgency?

We can't mourn Paris because it's convenient for us, and then forget about it later, just as we can't let islands and cultures disappear under the Pacific because we don't want to change our lifestyle. We can't ignore the problems—violence occurs every day in many forms, but we only choose to care about it sometimes.

The trouble is—there's no easy solution to end the violence that has destabilized the Middle East. There's no quick fix to the disenfranchisement of people living in Paris's *banlieues* or those traveling to Syria to join the ranks of ISIS. There's no replacement for the species and civilizations that have been and will be lost due to our warming climate.

But in the face of these big problems, we are presented with an opportunity to finally stand together and ask the difficult questions about why some people's livelihoods matter than others. We owe it to the victims who lost their lives watching a concert at the Bataclan, enjoying a drink on an evening terrace, or walking home along Paris's beautiful streets. We owe it to future generations to preserve our planet, trees, and ecosystem before there is nothing left. We owe to future generations to protect the streets of Paris, and other achievements of civilization, before they disappear under water.

We owe it to Paris to protect what the city begs us to appreciate every day: our humanity.

Greetings from Paradise

by Janine Oshiro

For Daneen Bergland

How is your heart? How is your hallux?
How is your inner sea horse?

How is your breathing? How is your ending?
What dust has your faded green rag picked up?

Everything's fine here. Like, hi. Like, hello.
Like, hey, we need to get together.

So how grows the chervil? How are the snails
in the clearing where you once grew potatoes?

How is your mother? How is your father?
How much longer can your hangnail hold on?

How is your daughter, who combs the curls
of pink little ponies and stones them to death?

How is the fruit rotting into wine in your basement?
How much meat have you managed to can?

How is the spiders' meditation retreat on the shelf
reserved for authors whose last names start with "Q"?

Do they chant, "Shanti, shanti, shanti, aum"
as the universal vacuum breathes them in?

Hi! Hi! Hello! I send you my love from paradise.
The water's fine. Why don't you join me?

I drowned a man in me, and today the tides
are unanimous in their stinging debris: the broken glass,

the gassy blobs of man o' wars scribbling their blue
signatures, the bees weighed down with salty wings.

I held him down, and he mouthed fine, fine.
He's grateful to float face down in the left atrium

of my spacious heart, beating for you, like a flipper
slapping at the water's surface: Life is so, so, so, so

beautiful: the whales' flocculent dumps float like
clouds reflecting the clouds until they dissipate.

What Lucy Feels Like

by Claudia Cortese

The air
inside a
leaf fist.
Not
October's
burnt romantics
or tin aftermath
of rain,
haiku's
mist through trees,
lone bonsai
on hillside green—
solitude's calm
is not the air
I mean.
When you feel
mad at
world
which means
mad at
self,
there's no
sweet alone.
Mid-summer sewer,
trash, rat dung
is the wind

I mean,
meaning—
I'm ugly
stupid
my cottage cheese
thighs
and bubble ankles
in one beige sock
one white.

That the mind isn't guided by the punished shade

by Tony Mancus

Dust in its emoting.
Adjust this crumb.

This numbness. Leaving us
to blank.

Spots on the surface. A dampness
somewhere nears us to sleep.

We walk on another kind
of nest for the body.

Swept up—pale
feathers, a bucket, bones.

Manger

by Suzanne Matson

So I'm with Rosalie at Girl Scouts, like every Wednesday, and I'm passing out the manger pieces I pre-cut with my jigsaw at home. That's what Karen loves about having a dad on board. I've got a jigsaw, and unlike Rolf, Karen's husband, I know how to use one. We've got only two more Wednesdays, counting this one, before Our Lady of Hope Elementary closes for Christmas break, so it's pretty important that we get these mangers put together now. While they're drying, the girls are going to use clay to make the Holy Family, the animals, the wise men and such. While *those* are drying, the girls will paint the mangers and glue straw in place. I didn't know how far we'd get today, but you can see that time was of the essence. Every minute of the troop meeting definitely counted. Plus, Rosalie's looked forward to this for a week. At home I let her put on the safety goggles and cut some of the manger walls, but I was glad when she got bored of that and wanted to watch *America's Next Top Model*. Some of those walls she cut were a little off. I'm a carpenter, and I'm kind of crazy about things lining up. When you're building, you can't just say, okay, close enough.

I was going around the room, showing the girls what a plumb line is, adjusting their corners into 90-degree angles, helping them see they could make something that would stand up. *Structural integrity*, I tell them. I build roofs over people's heads; they can't leak, and they can't go flying off in the next 50-year storm. This may be just a manger, but that's no reason for it to be half-assed. Half-assed is how I barely got through high school, how I fell into early marriage. I wasn't going to get into advanced stuff with the troop, but the point is, you don't frame a house with the wrong nail. Too long goes through; too short or too skinny doesn't hold; too fat splits the wood. A good 16-penny sinker, and you go straight, true, into the heart of the beam.

With the mangers, all you needed was a light coating of wood glue, accurate positioning, and patience. The girls were concentrating, and I was proud of them. My daughter was doing a good job; she'd gotten the three walls of the manger glued together and standing up, and was just about to lay on one side of the roof.

There was no reason Joyce had to show up just then to take Rosalie. Sure, it was her night to have the kids, due to our absolutely insane custody arrangement that yanked them back and forth in the middle of the week. I had primary custody because of Joyce living with her new boyfriend, but she had the kids Wednesday through Friday alternating with the weeks she had them Saturday-Sunday. I was not about to let her get them every weekend because weekends are important family time, and Joyce with her jerk-wad live-in boyfriend was not exactly the best atmosphere in the family department. But the arrangement sucked. I can't tell you how many times the kids would come home with zeros for homework on Joyce's Thursdays and Fridays. I keep a record of all the zeros under Joyce's watch and show them to my lawyer, Martin.

If Joyce sent me an email in the morning asking for Rosalie early, I certainly didn't get it in time. I'm not one of those people hanging out on email all day long. I'd gone from finishing the manger pieces at home, to working on Martin's bathroom remodel to pay down my tab with him, to being at the troop meeting. It's not my job to wonder if Joyce is going to try and screw over the normal arrangements so I should just keep checking email.

Rosalie is trying to get her walls to stop slipping when Joyce storms the library in her stiletto boots and fake fur vest and loud voice. She's always accused me of overpowering her because I'm 6'2" and she's 5'1", but let me tell you she's the one who fills up a room. Fills it up and sucks all the air out of it. Joyce and I are not even supposed to be within fifty feet of each other since the incident with the backpack, but here she is in the forbidden zone, and I can see it now, how she's going to file the complaint against me for being too near her.

Karen tries her best to get Joyce to go back to live parking and wait, but Joyce is ranting about how she needs to get Rosalie so she can get the kids over to her father's in time for some tickets they all have for a movie. Some stupid Christmas movie, in a theater, on a school night. I could see the homework zeros coming.

Excuse me Karen, but you shouldn't have to deal with this, I say, very polite. And here I am three feet away from Joyce, who loves to lie in court and tell the judge that I push her around—which I have never done once—so *I'm* supposed to keep fifty feet away from *her*. But here she is in my troop meeting.

Listen, Joyce, I say, calm as can be. Rosalie's not finished here, but when she is we'll send her out. Rest assured, we won't detain her. You'll get her on the dot at 4:30, just like you're supposed to.

I pause for a cleansing breath, like we do before Men's Circle, and I try to reframe: everything's good. I've got twelve credits left on my Associate's; Patrick made the Honor Roll, and Rosalie likes her new school counselor. This is about the kids, what I'm trying to create—structure and consistency, nothing I ever had, growing up.

Rosalie's not looking at either of us, just pinching her manger walls. She hasn't even had a chance to begin rolling out her Holy Family, though some of the other girls are already on their sheep. Joyce is going on in her loud voice about how she emailed and how this is a family activity and they already bought tickets and I tell her I don't give a shit about her tickets, which are probably going to make Rosalie get behind on her homework anyway.

That's when Joyce goes around me and tells Rosalie, get your stuff, we're leaving, and Rosalie looks from her mother to me in this way that breaks my heart but I'm fighting for her here, so I tell Joyce, she's not leaving, not until the troop meeting is finished, and Joyce picks up the backpack herself and grabs Rosalie by the elbow and of course that means that her hand jerks and the manger walls come apart.

This I cannot stand. My little girl has been holding onto those walls for a good ten minutes and in five more she was going to have a lasting bond. But now her time is wasted, and she will fall even further behind the other girls, and this is classic Joyce, wreck- ing her children's lives because she has a whim, because she wants to make up for her lack of attention to the small things with big, splashy, candy-coated good times.

So I take *her* by the elbow, and I say, you are leaving *now*, and she swings her pocket book at me. I step back and say to Karen, Did you see that? and her hand is to her mouth but she nods with- out speaking that yes she did see that. I grab Joyce by the elbow once more and have to hold tight so she doesn't pull that again, and I take the precaution of removing the purse from her other hand because that's the weapon, but when her one hand is free and mine are full she starts battering her little fist against my chest and that's when I hear Rosalie beginning to wail in the background. You fucking bitch, I say to Joyce, and of course I know that's wrong around the troop, and even more wrong in Our Lady of Hope, besides which this is not who I want to be, but there is only so much I can take from this woman. I'm trying to back away from her hammering fist before I snap, and that's when I bump into the craft table, hard, because I was moving sudden and I'm a big guy, and I hear the clattering of more mangers. God knows how many of them went down.

Will you look at what you did?—I admit—I yelled at her. Then she's screaming back how I'm a bully and I'm always pushing her around—yes, she's saying I'm pushing *her* around, which so help me God I have never done in my life—and then I see the cops in the doorway. Karen must have called them on her cell, or maybe a secretary looking in, but then Joyce is crying up a storm and rubbing her arm and pointing to me and before I know it, I'm cuffed. That's when I come apart like a mortar into shards, slivers, a hundred jagged pieces. I take my two hands cuffed together and twist free of the policeman, and yes, I do it, I flip the craft table over. All the little girls are crying. Rosalie is running from the room. And I—I am a man crucified. I am a man losing a child. I have become the disaster Rosalie will remember all her life, and probably in her dreams, watching herself trying and trying to put together the ruined pieces of her nativity.

The Synthetic Option

(Inspired by the BBC documentary 'Guys and Dolls')

WHIT TAYLOR

OVER THE COURSE OF A FEW MONTHS, OUR FILM CREW CONDUCTED A CHARACTER STUDY OF A MAN AND HIS RELATIONSHIP WITH HIS REALDOLL™.

REALDOLLS™ ARE THE WORLD'S MOST REALISTIC AND EXPENSIVE SEX DOLLS, PRODUCED IN A SMALL FACTORY IN CALIFORNIA.

THEY ARE CUSTOMIZABLE, AND AS SUCH, COME AT A STEEP PRICE OF $4,000+ DOLLARS.

IT IS BELIEVED THAT THEY PROVIDE PLEASURE AND COMPANY TO A FEW THOUSAND MEN AROUND THE WORLD.

HERE IS ONE SUCH STORY.

LET'S GO WAKE HER UP.

I'M PRETTY SURE SHE'S SLEEPIN'.
DO NOT DISTURB

DO NOT DISTURB

MORNIN' BABE.

I CHANGE HER FACE LIKE THIS EVERY MORNIN'.

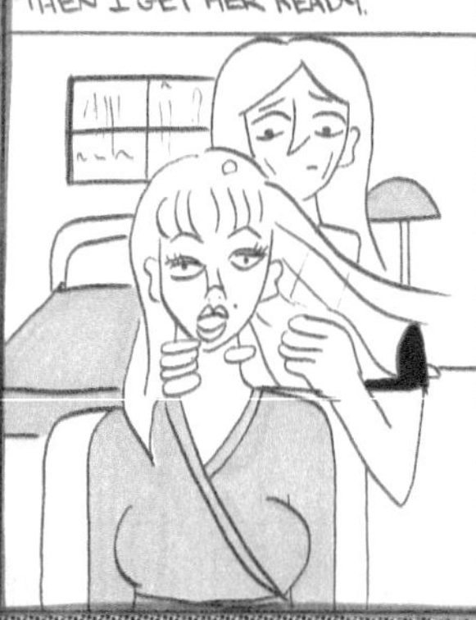

THEN I GET HER READY.

BELINDA'S CLASSY. I DON'T WANT HER LOOKIN' LIKE NO FLOOZY. LOOK LIKE A TRILLION PEOPLE DONE HAD HER. I DON'T WANT THAT.

AT FIRST IT WAS BONIN' 24/7, BUT NOW WE'VE DEVELOPED A DEEP PARTNERSHIP. SHE KNOWS WHAT I LIKE, RESPECTS THAT, AND LETS ME DO WHAT I WANT, WHEN I WANT.
DAMMIT.

TOMORROW I GOTTA SEND HER OFF TO GET FIXED. HER LIMBS IS GOTTEN LOOSE FROM ALL THAT FUN, BUT SHE COST ME A BUNDLE, SO I GOTTA TAKE GOOD CARE OF HER.

WHEN SHE GONE, I DON'T KNOW WHAT I'LL DO.
HANDLE WITH CARE

8AM

SHE SECURE?

I'VE BEEN OBSESSED WITH COLLECTIBLES OF ALL SORTS SINCE I WAS A KID. ESPECIALLY WIZARD ART

AND MY MA SAID WHENEVER SHE TOOK ME TO THE MALL, THAT I ALWAYS PLAYED WITH THE MANNEQUINS.

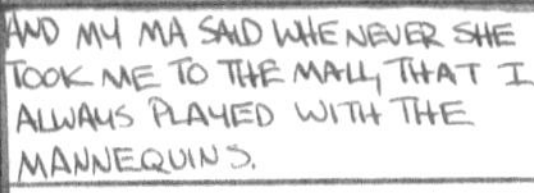

THEY GAVE ME A THRILL.

NOWADAYS, BELINDA AND I LEAD A QUIET LIFE

I COME HOME AFTER A DAY OF FRYIN' JALAPEÑO POPPERS AND ALL THAT GARBAGE AND WE SETTLE INTO WATCH 'THE SIMPSONS'. THAT SHOW MAKES US LAUGH.

AFTER DINNER I GO ROTATE MY WIZARD FIGURINES AND PLAY DRUM SET WHILE SHE HANGS OUT TILL BEDTIME.

I LOOK FORWARD TO NIGHT TIME: THE MINDBLOWIN' LOVIN' AND CUDDLIN'.
READ THE SIGN GENTLEMAN. IT ABOUT TO GET ALL X-RATED UP IN HERE.
DO NOT DISTURB
SOMETIMES, ON THE WEEKENDS, WE DO PHOTO SHOOTS IN THE YARD.
SHE LOOKS GREAT IN ARMY FATIGUES, DON'T SHE?
SEE, I LIKE THE WAY SHE HOLDIN' THAT AK-47 LIKE SHE MEAN BUSINESS.
I DON'T REALLY TAKE HER OUT IN PUBLIC THOUGH FOR OBVIOUS REASONS. HECK, OUTSIDE OF MY JOB, I STAY TO MYSELF.
I USED TO TRY TO GO OUT INTO THE OUTSIDE WORLD, BUT PEOPLE LOOK AT ME FUNNY.
YOU'VE GOT MAIL
I GET IT. I GOT ACNE SCARS AND BAD TEETH. MAN, PEOPLE IS SURFACE.
I HAD AN ORGANIC GIRLFRIEND ONCE. HER NAME WAS NANCY.
SEE, THIS HER PICTURE.
DON'T KNOW WHY I KEEP IT. MAYBE TO REMIND ME NEVER TO GO DOWN THAT ROAD AGAIN.
SHE AIN'T APPRECIATE ME FOR ME.
PLUS, THERE WAS THAT PARTY...

SURPRISE!

I THOUGHT YOU HAD JUST ONE.

NAH, I GOT A FEW, BUT BELINDA MY MAIN GIRL. OUTSIDE OF YOU OF COURSE.

AND YOU USE ALL OF THEM?

NOT ALL AT ONCE.

WELL, THAT ENDED THAT. BUT IT'S OK. SAVES ME FROM BUYING VALENTINE'S DAY PRESENTS.

I ENDED UP SELLIN' THEM OTHER DOLLS FOR A PRETTY PENNY AND BOUGHT ME A NICE SUIT OF ARMOR. WANNA SEE?

DO NOT DISTURB

NICE, RIGHT?

SO YEAH.

WELL, THAT ABOUT IT FOR TODAY. THINK I'M GONNA GO TAKE A NAP.

OVER THE NEXT MONTH, CECIL REQUESTED THAT WE NOT TAPE HIM, AS HE EXPLAINED THAT HE WAS IN A "DARK PLACE".

WE RESPECTED HIS WISHES.

ONE MONTH LATER
WELL, DELIVERY TRUCK SHOULD BE HERE ANY MOMENT. I CAN'T WAIT. GONNA BE LIKE A SECOND HONEYMOON.
HANDLE WITH CARE
WELL GODDAMN.
EXCUSE US.
SLAM!
DO NOT DISTURB
DO NOT DISTURB

SECOND HONEYMOON INDEED. WITHOUT BELINDA, I WAS A MAN LOST, BUT NOW I AM REBORN.
I RATHER BE LOCKED IN AN IGLOO IN THE ARCTIC, NAKED AND HUNGRY, THAN BE WITHOUT MY GIRL.
I'M FEELIN' SO INSPIRED, I THINK WE GONNA GO FOR A DAY TRIP.
YUH SEE, I DON'T USUALLY BRING HER OUT OF THE HOUSE. EXCEPT FOR LAWNMOWER RIDES AND THEM PHOTO SHOOTS, BECAUSE PEOPLE GIVE ME FUNNY LOOKS.
IN CASE THEY THINK SHE GONE CATATONIC, I DONE MADE A BADGE FOR HER WHICH SAYS SHE OK.
HELLO MY NAME IS BELINDA
WILLOW BROOK POND RECREATION PARK
HERE WE ARE AT THE DUCK POND. I THOUGHT IT'D BE NICE TO SPOIL HER WITH A PICNIC.
YOU LIKE THEM PLUM, DON'T YOU?
SEE, SHE LIKE HAND-FRUITS, NO BERRIES OR ANY OF THAT NONSENSE. EVEN THOUGH I GOTTA HOLD 'EM FOR HER

I HEAR THAT THERE ARE MEN ALL OVER THE WORLD WHO BUY THESE DOLLS AND IT MAKES PERFECT SENSE.
BRENDA

BUT MOSTLY, WELL, I PUT IT LIKE THIS: ALL HUMAN RELATIONSHIPS IS TEMPORARY.

I MEAN, THEY FEEL REAL, YOU KNOW, WHEN YOU DOIN' EM, PLUS THEY PRETTY.

PEOPLE COME AND GO OUT OF YOUR LIFE, FRIENDS AND ROMANCES END.
Y'KNOW I KNOW IT AIN'T MUCH, BUT I WAS WONDERIN'...

FOLKS BETRAY YOU. ONE MINUTE YOU'RE TAKING A SHOWER TOGETHER, THE NEXT, THEY A COMPLETE STRANGER.
IF YOU'D DO ME THE HONOR OF MARRYIN' ME?

OH YEAH, AND THERE'S A THING CALLED DEATH.

I THOUGHT THAT'S WHAT YOU'D SAY.

PEOPLE MIGHT THINK I'M GOING TO HELL FOR MY LIFESTYLE, BUT I DON'T GIVE A RAT'S ASS.

BELINDA AND ME? SEE, THAT'S FOREVER. WE GONNA TURN TO EARTH TOGETHER.

WHAT YOU LOOKIN' AT? MIND YOUR OWN BUSINESS!

AND THAT'S HEAVEN TO ME.

Fin.

Toast

by Gus Rancatore & Corky White

K yoto's Kamo River, in English, translates as Duck River. Modern bridges cross the wide, somewhat shallow stream, but a child or intrepid adult can also use a series of small stone turtle-shapes, hopping from islet to islet, moving from one side of the city to the other. Water birds with wide wingspans circle in widening gyres. We're here so one of us, Corky, can show the other, Gus, the Japan she loves after many years of visiting and studying, working as an anthropologist.

Japan can seem like a fantasy version of a country like the imagined Ireland, or the Brigadoon village appearing once every century. Trees have ropes around their trunks to remind people of a special spirit. Once I saw what might have been birdhouses that seemed scattered along the roadside. They were explained as homes for *kami*, or spirits. Houses and streets may be guarded by *tanuki*, ceramic badger-like mischief figures wearing hip flasks of sake and sporting oversized testicles.

At 8:30am we are off in search of a cafe-style Japanese breakfast. The Japanese breakfast is a small thing done well, with revealing expressions of localism, similar to the French café au lait and croissant or the espresso and cornetto of Italy. Japanese breakfast is an incentive and reward for those who start the day earlier. For visitors it is a short introduction to the small surprises that please and instruct foreigners. Japan is, unexpectedly, "a toast paradise."

A few blocks east of the Kamo and its hovering birds we park our bikes on a street crowded with purposeful pedestrians and bike and auto traffic. We enter Gogo, an older, comfy, sepia-toned cave of a café inhabited by older and comfy regulars. A calmly industrious woman takes orders, which rarely vary. Everyone gets the coffee and toast combo, which the Japanese call "morning set-to," or "morning service."

Every shop offers small distinctions in service. At Gogo the toast is amazing: evenly browned, crisp on top, soft inside, embuttered and yielding to your bite. It is accompanied by well-made coffee, a boiled egg and a tiny salad of shredded cabbage. The slices are thick, here cut in thirds to make what the British call "toast soldiers," strips of toast with which to dip out the yolk from the soft-boiled egg. The toast is very ordinary, very wonderful and profoundly Japanese. And the British might say, "so very more-ish."

The toast is Japanese in that it strives for perfection of a borrowed preparation. In the same way, pizza has recently been localized in Japan merely by perfecting the perfect Italian – by attempting to meet essential Neapolitan ideals, and then surpassing those standards. Japan has had great French restaurants, great Italian restaurants and now a trend in perfectionism has resulted in perfect pizza. One Tokyo pizza maker has won prizes in Naples. Ordinary pizza in Japan might display squid ink or chopped *shiso* leaf (an aromatic herb). It can be dressed with corn and pineapple and proclaimed "Hawaiian." But these pizzas are essentially Japanese. They exist in dialogue and in tension with foreign traditions and they have earned the seal of approval from the commune di Napoli, "la vera pizza napoletana." There is a shop in Naples that sells

New York Style pizza. There should be one selling Tokyo Style pizza.

Toast in Japan is ubiquitous enough not to be noticed. Bread has been around a long time in Japan. It first came with the Portuguese missionaries and traders who arrived in the sixteenth century. In the early seventeenth century a book of recipes from Spain and Portugal was published in Japan, the "barbarians' cookbook." In it, guides to baking, involving applying heat from above and below introduced European techniques to Japan. The recipe itself is suggestive rather than specific: "knead flour with sweet sake and allow it to rise. Cover with a heavy blanket and after it has risen, cook it." Other Portuguese baked goods such as *casutera*, a sweet cake named for the town of Castille, with eggs and sugars added are glossed in the 18th century as "confectionery." The Portuguese are also credited with "katsu" or "cutlet" –the breadcrumb-crusted fried pork chop or filet and the bread from which panko breadcrumbs are made. At the time, bread was a very exotic preparation, but now, no one will suggest that "pan" (from the Portuguese word for bread, "pao") or for that matter, casutera, is not Japanese.

Sitting in Gogo, we are the only curly-haired customers as she explains Japanese food-ways. When Christianity seemed to threaten the soul of Japan, most missionaries were driven out. Those who stayed introduced useful items like matchlock guns, produced in Portuguese India on the island of Goa and brought to Japan in 1543. Trade was still permitted, but restricted to a tiny manmade island in Nagasaki harbor, called Deshima, where French and Dutch traders were permitted to conduct business. The Japanese had considerable curiosity about foreign things, and "Dutch leaning" (*rangaku*) attracted young elites to study western medicine and military science.

The Portuguese had coffee – later to be the partner of toast in a Japanese breakfast. When Dutch traders provided coffee in the

1640s it was first thought to be a medicine. One Nagasaki magistrate said, "It's made from burned black beans and it tastes dreadful." The Dutch traders' taste for coffee spread from low to high, from the prostitutes they frequented who found it useful to keep themselves awake so customers might not slink off without paying, to the Shinto priests at Dazaifu in Kyushu, where a Japanese merchant brought it as an offering to the gods.

Coffee was to become the key public social experience, taking the place of tea as a more modern public beverage. The *chaya*, or tea house, provided a social space where gatherings of friends were flavored by tea, but the chaya disappeared as coffee cafes proliferated. The *chaya* did not serve coffee, and the café does not serve green tea. The first cafes, appearing in the Meiji era, in about 1888, were styled after the leather-chaired, tobacco-scented masculine coffeehouses of New York and London. By the early twentieth century, Japan was Brazil's first targeted overseas market, and cafes proliferated. Some decades later, Japan became the third largest importer of coffee, which became ubiquitous by way of the new cafes, with at least one on every city block in Tokyo and Osaka by the Second World War. The cafes provided the social space that became absolutely necessary for merchants, students, *flaneurs*, flappers and literati.

Toast had appeared in cafes in the early twentieth century, but its popularity was boosted by U.S.-donated wheat flour which flooded post-war Japan during the Allied occupation. Bread clearly now had a central place in the Japanese diet. School lunches now contained bread instead of rice, and a breakfast at home might now have toast and cereal instead of rice and miso soup, since a traditional breakfast demands more preparation time and since most adults, both male and female, now work outside the home. Bread has long settled in everywhere, and regional variations of the café "morning service" or "set" have become objects of local pride.

Some food tourists in Japan ride certain trains to enjoy the *ekibento* (station lunchboxes) of different towns. People who enjoy "toast tourism" visit places like Nagoya, a city to the northwest of Tokyo to enjoy its morning sets. The sumptuous café breakfasts, called "Nagoya morning" can include all manner of foods: macaroni salad, breakfast meats, smoked fish, French toast and a prize dish —Nagoya ogura toast, covered with sweet azuki bean jams, accompanied by yogurt and topped with fresh fruit. Fortified by this breakfast you could visit the Nagoya branch of Boston's Museum of Fine Arts.

Retired people on fixed incomes often wait until the end of the day's morning service and arrive just before its conclusion, around 11 a.m., to feast on what can then be their lunch, at very low cost. The massive size of these morning feasts seems to contradict images of aesthetic proportionality and delicacy in Japanese food.

The 1980s, the booming period now called the "bubble years," saw the development of a "normal" café set – coffee (or black tea, never green tea in a cafe) plus toast, an egg, and almost always a small bowl of shredded cabbage, carrots and a cherry tomato, sometimes with the peel cut to resemble rabbit ears. You could also have scrambled eggs, waffles, pancakes and croissants (in addition to the toast) and a hot Danish pastry with ice cream.

The bread that becomes perfect Japanese toast is usually white, but artisanality in all things has achieved stunning variety in the bread experiences of Japan, from hand-kneaded multi-grain and seeded varieties to the lightest of *shokupan*, or white, silky, marshmallow loaves—just made for the caramelization of toasting. You learn a lot about the power of the Maillard effect from toast.

Aiming at the best, micro-bakeries produce a few excellent loaves a day. Like sushi in the film *Jiro Dreams of Sushi* or ramen in the film, *Tampopo*, bread can become the object of serious attention (called "*kodawari*") for makers and connoisseurs. *Kodawari* is a word to conjure with: it can mean "perfectionism" or "diligence" or "passion for what you do" in any craft or pursuit. In bread it reaches great heights but sometimes you have to hunt for it.

In Kyoto most people ride bicycles on sidewalks. Down a bustling street we wobbled our bikes to the left onto a smaller lane, and from there took another turn onto a cracked paved alley, at the very end of which is a dirt road with a wooden obelisk marked with the infinity sign. We followed that to another dirt path, left our bikes and approached a small, dilapidated farmhouse, incongruously abandoned in the middle of a major metropolitan city. A mysterious, Repo Man-like figure welcomed us and explained that he was growing herbs, and then disappeared again, into the shrubbery.

We slid open the outside door, proceeded in to the *genkan* (entrance area) where we placed our shoes out of the cluttered way and opened the interior door, calling out something polite like "gomen kudasai" (excuse me) and Mr. Yokota emerged from the kitchen wiping his hands on a towel.

We are there for the bread, and perhaps we are early, meaning between eleven and noon. Yokota-san's bread is made almost daily but in small quantities, depending on the availability of the right (organic, small batch) flours, the generosity of air-borne yeasts and his energy. If he makes ten loaves it is a productive day. Taught in Japan by Austrian and German friends, Yokota bakes breads that are tight, dense, and full of seeds and nuts. They slice up very thinly and their moist density means they stay alive longer – if you can resist eating it all at once.

The choices are few but intense: get a coriander rye or a fig bread, or a campagne made with graham flour. We stay for lunch. Yokota-san makes a delectable "lunch set"; open face sandwiches on his bread and a delicious soup (du jour, usually vegetable). Adding to the experience is the café area, with a capacity of about eight at a long, low table. We sit on *zabuton* (flat pillows). We watch the light through the large window on the "natural" (read: unkempt) garden. The silent, welcoming gardener is not to be seen. This is perhaps the most calming experience of food that can be imagined: the light is indirect, the mood serene.

More European influence is seen in the perfect croissants of Japan – even in chain bakeries such as Patisserie Donq, a bakery founded in Japan in 1906, a branch of which we encountered on another bike ride in Kyoto. Corky first went to Japan in the mid-1960s, and, never having been to France and untried in the arts of French *boulangerie*, still knew a good croissant the moment she ate her first Donq and dipped it in her first (Japanese) nutty boule de café au lait. It remains in her memory as her finest French food moment, though she has been to Paris many times.

We travel with the dictate of Calvin Trillin in our minds: there are no established meals, only eating experiences separated by the time it takes to get from one to the next. Brushing off the flakey crumbs of these croissants, we arrive at another café for its morning set, and the toast of the morning. These white milk-and-cream slices are not industrial Wonder or Sunbeam, but they do inspire nostalgia for mid-century American childhoods when even those breads, slathered with margarine, made us happy.

Recently, missing those toasts we settled in at a Korean café in Boston where lessons learned from Japan show up, as is often true, shouted loudly: here the toast was 3-4 inches tall, called "brick toast," and soaked with caramel syrup and topped with maple syrup, resembled the thick sweet Bostocks of French patisseries even more than they do the real, quietly wonderful, toast of Japan.

NOW, IT IS JOY THAT IS PROHIBITED —
THE THING THAT ESCAPES ALL
ECONOMIES

by Kara Candito

OH NO YOU'RE NOT SUPPOSED
TO SAIL THE DRAKE PASSAGE
IN A WALNUT SHELL OR FOLLOW
THE PERUVIAN PRESIDENT'S
DAUGHTER ON TWITTER JUST
FOR THE PICTURES OF MORRISSEY
HER BELOVED WEIMARANER
OH JUST RESIST BEING A KNOWITALL
WHEN YOUR HUSBAND SAYS
LOOK HERE AT THIS MILITARY
EQUESTRIAN STATUE OF PIZARRO
SEE HOW ONE HOOF IS RAISED?
IT MEANS HE WAS WOUNDED
IN BATTLE OH NO DO NOT GOOGLE
THE MILITARY EQUESTRIAN STATUE
OF BOLIVAR IN LA PLAZA BOLIVAR
AND SAY HAHAHA BOTH HOOVES
ARE IN THE AIR AND BOLIVAR DIED
OF CONSUMPTION OH ALL RIGHT
IT'S OKAY TO SAY HAHAHA THE MILITARY
EQUESTRIAN STATUE OF PIZARRO
RUSTS ON THE SHORE OF THE RIVER RIMAC
A SORRY ASS STREAM OF TRASH
WHERE VULTURES SHIT AND DOGS DIE

AND YES EVERYONE CAN SHOUT JUST ONCE
OUT OUT CONQUISTADOR!
LET'S MELT IT DOWN LET'S TURN IT
INTO A WALNUT SHELL AND SAIL
ALL THE WAY TO ALICANTE

Congo: The Story of One Family's Endurance

by Lisa Shannon

An excerpt from Mama Koko and the 100 Gunmen

Out of our puttering five-seater charter plane, Francisca and I looked down eight thousand or so feet to Congo below. Above the land leading to Dungu, vast blankets of the Congo basin forest stretched to the horizon in all directions, rivers slicing through, catching the sunlight. The canopy was too thick to see through, leaving what was beneath entirely to the imagination, aside from a couple of mining towns and tiny settlements on remote bends in the river.

It had been a year of bad news since the day Francisca got the first call from home, the day after Kony's attacks started. She was tired, distracted, spending almost every night up, trying to get through to her family for news, unhinged by the media reports intermittently firing across the international wires, mixed with static-marred cell phone calls from home. Sometimes she could talk for a minute or two before the line cut out. Sometimes, in the middle of the night, after she had finally gotten to sleep, her phone would ring and, panicked, she'd jump out of bed and run to answer it, her hands shaking so much that she fumbled when she tried to pick up, hitting the wrong buttons.

Occasionally, Francisca's calls made it through to her brothers or Mama Koko, when they weren't spending months at a time hiding in the bush. No one had died the day she heard gunshots and the line went dead, but that was little consolation. Every call yielded broken, hasty reports of gunmen and cousins, nieces, nephews, and more cousins killed, abducted, burned alive on Christmas Day.

* * *

On the ground in Dungu, after Francisca's long embraces with her dear ones, we drove across Dungu to Mama Koko's place. It was a one-story road-front cement house, dripping with bright orange climbers. It stood just one block from the Dungu Bridge, the gateway to the Bamokandi neighborhood, which was the site of the in-town attack and LRA sighting earlier that day.

André and Bernadette had bought the land more than half a century before, but long gone were their shop's shelves of household goods and cases of beer. The land was now only half hers, and not by choice. It sat right on the main junction, next to a roundabout crowned with a statue of a native warrior, marking the fork in two roads heading north. Because of the house's strategic position on the road and its strong cement walls, the Congolese army kicked the family out when it suited them, and of late, that was often. The family had moved back in only four days before our arrival.

We slipped inside the three-bedroom house, where extended-family members squished together politely in the living room, watching Francisca, Mama Koko, and me feast on an astounding by-request vegan meal: pumpkin-seed dumplings, fried bananas, homemade soy milk, brown rice with cooked cassava leaves known as *pondu*, bean stew, and sweet pineapple.

But it was a welcome feast among ruins. Devastation hung in the air, like the gunshots everyone heard earlier that day. The children crowded around us, watching keenly as we ate the elaborate spread, mamas chastising them to stand back. The children ate only one meal a day, and this wasn't it.

Everything had changed. All of the treasured household items were stolen when the Congolese army took over. Mama Koko stashed their remaining good dishes and furniture with friends on the other side of town. She didn't replace them. She didn't keep anything nice anymore. She knew they would be taken, again.

After we ate, we resettled into the backyard *yapu*, a large open-air hut made of palm leaves and adobe, furnished with traditional woven lounge chairs and wooden coffee tables. This was the real living room on the property, where kids played, women cooked, and guests were welcomed.

André's grave sat off to the side, with a couple of other family tombs, large coffin-shaped cement blocks graced with rainbow pinwheels and the wires of decapitated plastic flowers cemented into cans in place of a headstone. Francisca had brought these love-gifts from America to honor the family members who died when she was so far away, but the plastic flowers had long ago been lifted by grave robbers. Only the rainbow pinwheels remained, spinning cheerfully in the breeze.

The rest of the sprawling property, well over an acre in size, was dotted with traditional adobe huts for family and squatters. Mama Koko lived in the back in a traditional hut, not in the cement house.

In the yapu, family gathered in a loose circle and small talk lurched along—how big the children had grown, the new babies born—and soon Mama Koko and the rest were hungry to share, their minds and tongues fixed on the in-town massacre only days before. Francisca stalled, asking after neighbors and old friends. She had always avoided blood and gore: When she was a kid, she wouldn't kill a goat or hen like her brothers and sisters did. Back in Portland, Kevin always came home from the video store with *his* and *hers* movies: an action flick for himself and a smooth comedy for Francisca. While he watched his shoot-ups, she roamed the house in self-imposed exile. She couldn't look at that stuff. She knew they were only movies, but she cried every time someone was killed.

That first afternoon in Dungu, the family wanted to talk. Some sat close to Francisca and held her hand. Francisca wasn't ready. She didn't want to know the details yet, what had been stolen, what they'd never get back, as if putting off the full report could make it less real. She wanted home to still be home.

It was easier for her to steer the conversation toward me, the guest. In the United States, we often lead with the question *"What do you do?"* In Congo, they lead with *"Who is your family?"* In my case, they asked: Was I married? Did I have children?

Francisca answered on my behalf: "Someone just wrote about Lisa in a big newspaper in the US," she said, referring to an article that Nicholas Kristof had written in the *New York Times* about my complete life makeover and sudden foray into activism for the Congo. "She was engaged, but she had to choose between her fiancé and Congo. She chose Congo."

The family was quiet for a moment, processing this oddity. Then her cousin declared, "So it is like *that* you are a Congolese woman!"

Everyone laughed.

But we couldn't stop the current. Everyone else—the extended family packed into the family *yapu*—jumped in to share bits about the in-town attack down the road just days before.

The day of the attack, a few children were collecting water after school, at the community faucet in plastic jugs. They spotted men in long coats with guns. LRA. The children ran. The gunmen followed and started shooting. A bullet hit a father carrying his three-year-old. It flew through his arm and pierced his daughter's stomach, blowing her intestines out the other side.

They shot a young woman running with her one-year-old baby boy, ripping apart her genitalia. She collapsed. Grasping the baby, she dragged herself on her back into the bushes to hide.

The United Nations didn't send scouts that night to look for survivors, even though they were only a few miles up the road and it wasn't even dark yet when the attack happened. No Congolese army patrols, either.

In the morning, a neighbor followed the bloody trail to the bushes, where they found her dead body. She had bled out during the night.

Her baby was cradled in her lifeless arms, still nursing.

Francisca's mind was racing as brothers and cousins jumped in, talking over each other in a chorus of details.

I asked the family if they knew the mother and baby.

Yes. Francisca's eyes widened when she heard the name.

It was Antoinette, Francisca's cousin.

Lucky Jews

by Erica Lehrer

Fortune and misfortune are neighbors.
– German proverb

A tiny Jewish head, wearing a fur-trimmed hat, rolled across the lace tablecloth in a Kraków apartment. It was stopped by a pack of Marlboros. The gaze pointed toward a disjoined arm. A miniature hand clutched a curling scrap of Torah parchment lined with painstakingly flourished Hebrew letters. Assembled, the figurine stood about five inches tall on springed legs. I touched it. It *shokled*, rocking in the characteristic posture of Jewish prayer.

As an anthropologist and the child of a Jewish refugee from Nazi Europe, I had begun to interview carvers in the late 1990s in the context of my research on Poland's Jewish heritage industry. I found my way to them mostly through shopkeepers who sold their wares; but one dear friend told me that his uncle used to make Jewish figurines. I asked if I could speak to him, and soon found myself at his dining room table, looking down at this disquieting array.

In the 1960s, my friend's carver uncle had discovered a Torah scroll hidden in the rafters of his father's house. Not an uncommon find in postwar Poland, the scroll was stashed there during the war by a doomed Jewish neighbor. Over the years, the carver would clip small squares from the scroll and put them in the hands of his sculptures, the better they should pray. He remembered his Jewish neighbors: the nearby farmer and his geese, the fellow Boy Scout who shared Passover matzo with him. He stopped cutting the Torah scroll in the 1990s after an Israeli tourist told him he was doing something sacrilegious; by the time we met, he had turned to photocopying. Figurines in his personal collection still held the original Hebrew texts, often upside down. He chuckled softly: "I can never remember which way they go."

It could be said that in Poland today there are more Jewish figurines than Jews; indeed, most people living in Poland have never met a Jew. But nowadays, Poles live in towns and cities where Jews once made up 30% or more of the population. In many places, not a trace is left of the Jewish communities that once lived there. That blank space is filled today with images of Jews: figurines, pictures, magnets, postcards, and more. "Lucky Jews"—figurines and images of Jews holding money—have proliferated with particular potency in Poland along with the country's transition to capitalism. These good luck charms hang in homes and sit by cash registers in shops and restaurants across the country. In the context of debates about Polish complicity in Holocaust and post-Holocaust violence against Jews, and with a new influx of foreign Jews "returning" to Poland in a surge of secular pilgrimage, they have become a source of controversy.

On my journeys to Poland in the last two decades—part scholarly inquiry, part personal quest—the figurines have been a constant companion. They bear burdens disproportionate to their small size. To an outsider's eye, especially a Jewish one, their negative valences can be painfully obvious. They are easy to dismiss as material manifestations of Polish antisemitism. Not only because they traffic in stereotypes, but also by the simple fact of them: little wooden Jews where so much flesh and blood once thrived. They got under my skin.

I began seeking out their sources and tracing their travels. Who sold them? Who bought them? Why? And who made them? The figurines—with and without coins, church-fair toys and plaintive sculptures—showed up in the unlikeliest locations, with unexpected owners. In and around these objects unseen layers of cultural intimacy and emotion revealed themselves; they trade in timeworn stereotypes, but also carry traces of history, traumatic memory, and unspoken nostalgia for makers and buyers—Jews and non-Jews alike.

The Kraków hotel I stayed in for years turned out to have a life-sized wooden Jew playing a double bass tucked away behind the reception desk, and a portrait of a Jew counting money on the wall in the basement. A Warsaw butcher shop displayed a *shochet* (Jewish kosher butcher) figurine during the height of Poland's 2013 dispute concerning a government ban on ritual slaughter. Wooden Jews stand watch over bathroom fixtures in a Warsaw hardware store, and Jew-with-a-coin portraits hang as décor suggestions in suburban home improvement megastores. I have seen them displayed in Polish homes among menorahs and Torah pointers, as well as alongside figurines of Jesus and medieval Polish knights. They mingle with imported kosher groceries in the Chabad-Lubavitch shop in Krakow's Izaak synagogue, and by star-of-David pendants in the nearby Galicia Jewish Museum. I have also stumbled across them far from their birthplace, in Israeli, American, and Australian Jewish homes; on a scholar's shelf between academic tomes in Hebrew; accompanying Polish-Jewish ancestors' photos on a retirement community filing cabinet; by *kiddush* cups and sabbath candlesticks on a suburban credenza. I was surprised by the range of sentiments they evoked, even among their owners and creators.

The figurines are not a flash in the pan; no made-in-Taiwan bauble hot-stamped "Kraków" in place of "Rome" for a newly booming tourist market. Miniature Jews have deep roots in Polish culture—emerging in different forms over more than a century. They appeared alongside other local characters as puppets in pre-war Christian passion plays and as toys in Easter fairs, and later as secular sculptures sold in Cold War socialist folk art outlets. In the postwar era, they took on a de facto memorial quality when the Jews on which they were modeled had suddenly and violently disappeared. A checkered history underlies their newer forms and current popularity.

I came away from my search for figurines less sure of any singular meaning. Yet I was fascinated by what these small objects *do*. They not only separate, but connect Poles and Jews in ways not visible to the naked eye. They are instruments to express meanings, relationships, and emotions that find no other ready form or venue. They provoke the most various of reflections: A Polish Catholic woman told me that when the Nazis invaded in 1939, her father threw their Jewish figurines into the fire out of fear. A Jewish Holocaust survivor in Kraków commissioned figurines from a village carver as a corrective to those he saw as terribly stereotypical—though the distinction was lost on me. Conversations with Poles about the figurines in their homes led more than once to roundabout disclosures of their own Jewish roots.

Yet Jews and Poles each tend to understand the figurines only within their own familiar cultural framework, unaware of their meanings to the other. Jews wax nostalgic about a pre-war Jewish Poland that Tevye-and-Chagall-like fiddler figurines evoke, but cannot comprehend—or bristle at the thought—that Poles might do the same. And many Poles are simply puzzled that Jews, faced with figurines holding gold coins, see them as anything but an honorific: a celebration of Jewish entrepreneurship. Poles err by viewing the figurines naively, without reference to a long history of anti-Jewish imagery in which these objects inevitably partake; many Jews fail to see them as anything *but* antisemitism.

Given Poland's complex and ultimately tragic Jewish history, one would hope that such potent, problematic objects would be treated thoughtfully in Polish museums—some of which have impressive collections of them. Yet they are presented disappointingly, naively: as part of a vanished village culture alongside painted eggs and Easter palm fronds; just one more curiosity of quaint Slavic peasant life, free from politics or the complex history of Polish-Jewish coexistence. The figurines' increasingly vibrant presence–they are sold today in shops on the streets surrounding such museums–is also nowhere acknowledged.

So began my involvement as a student and curator of these provocative objects. I developed a museum exhibit—and eventually a book and website—that would present the figurines in a way that would evoke their historical complexity and "in-between" existence at the highly trafficked intersection of Polish, Jewish and also German cultures and communities—shaped today by a new social network of tourists, collectors, mourners, and devotees. I wanted to disrupt any simplistic or unitary view of their meaning, without neutralizing their disturbing qualities. In the exhibit I included a broad range of forms and genres of Poland's Jewish figurines emerging from different historical moments and sub-cultural contexts, yet all extending into the present. My goal was to display these diverse objects side-by-side and pose questions about ethnic sameness and difference; intercultural connections and distance; continuity and change in images of other cultural groups, and the deep roots of present-day stereotypes. I also wanted visitors—Poles and Jews in particular—to reflect on their own habits of thought and perception.

Does the historically shifting array of miniature Jews represent an underlying continuity, and if so, does that say something essential and unchanging about how Poles see Jews? Are Jew-with-a-coin talismans an entirely distinctive phenomenon, or just a late-capitalist expression of an always-magical Jew? Do the echoes of medieval biblical aspersions or Nazi propaganda visible in some figurines—the hunched back, the hooked nose, the cloth sack with coins—mean that they are antisemitic, even if their owners insist they mean to honor Jewish entrepreneurship by displaying them? Do figurine makers today ply their trade exclusively for mercenary reasons? Are their customers unsophisticated and oblivious? Can these figurines mean whatever we want them to mean, or is history encoded in their very forms? I tried to arrange the exhibit to confront viewers with these questions, and challenged them to formulate their own answers.

The role of curator offered wonderful possibilities for such productive provocation. Juxtaposing the venerable Polish "pensive Christ" with a similarly thoughtful everyday Jew suggested one artist's meditation on common religious roots. As the matching profiles of an everyday Jew and a bishop figurine made by a single carver of Emaus Easter toys reveal, in this particular case there was no distinct Jewish caricature; both figures sway and bobble in a shared technology of amusement. And the pairing of carver Maciej Manowiecki's capote-and-tallit-wearing Jew with his similarly black-and-white penguin is at once a humorous and unsettling commentary on the place of the Jew in the ecosystem of tourist tchotchkes.

Grouping together a wide array of postwar sculptures highlights both their individual and their mythical characteristics: the frequency with which figurines display hunchbacks, for example, reflects Christian cosmology's equating of Jewishness with moral failing, rather than neighborly observation. A 19th-century figural beehive in the shape of a Hasid prompts us to set today's plasticine souvenirs in a broader sweep of folk expression.

Traditional texts illustrate how the stereotype of the Jew as visualized in material form is reinforced in language—written, spoken, and sung. Józef Reguła's bas-reliefs based on Jewish jokes are one such illustration, as are traditional lyrics from the "Herods" or Christmas crèche plays in which the Jew is a central character. The centuries old traditional text—reproduced here in a 2013 version from a Polish cultural revitalization project—illustrates both the physical and character traits associated with the Jew, as well as the undercurrents of violence that both threatened and perhaps continue to threaten him.

The figurines are vastly enriched when we appreciate them as the product of individual human hands. Viewing them alongside the voices of their makers can be inspiring but also troubling, revealing motivations both profound and superficial. Numerous times I heard Jews say that a Jewish person would never make such a figurine; in response, I included Jewish figurines from the U.S. and Israel that belie that notion. And for good measure, I added African-American and Native American figurines from North America to remind Western and New World critics that those who would point fingers have their own landscape of painful ethnic "memorabilia" to face.

The exhibit catalyzed some of the discussions I had hoped for. In the gallery question books, people described their shock at confronting the figurines *en masse*; some expressed distress while watching video clips of casually antisemitic comments made by Polish collectors, and others dismissed my critical approach entirely, seeing in it evidence of typical Jewish self-obsession and oversensitivity. For the companion book, I commissioned short essays by Polish intellectuals, who treated the figurines from a range of viewpoints; some highlighting the failings of Polish national self-scrutiny in the aftermath of the Holocaust, some the ways in which unresolved Jewish historical trauma or cultural anxieties may color our perceptions of them.

Ultimately, I hope *Lucky Jews* establishes that Poland's Jewish figurines represent a special kind of "post-Jewish" cultural fragment, worthy of sustained consideration, and that museums should be leaders in cultural criticism by leveraging the difficult histories hidden in their own collections. In contrast to the domestic objects, buildings, or cemeteries left behind by this destroyed community, the figurines testify not only to centuries-long Jewish presence in Polish lands, but also the central place Jews continue to play in Polish collective consciousness. While they may embody pernicious cultural stereotypes, these figurines are also a wordless working through of history's wounds—linking debates about the difficult past and the everyday present in our homes, shops, and streets.

Visit the accompanying website: www.luckyjews.com

Switch or Axe

by Michael Walsh

Because someone has to go back, I return
to that boy showering unaware of his stepdad
listening at the bathroom door with its little hook
for the lock. The man decides he's had it
with the wife's kid, it's time to get a stick.
Get out now, I tell the boy, daydreaming
of his crush on another, get dressed,
grab your smokes, a change of clothes,
the phone number of someone you love
who's not related, run. Whether he can hear
right then doesn't matter. One day
he'll understand who he had to save.

I follow that stepdad with the plan
outside to the spring trees bending green.
I tell him, dead fifteen years now,
I found a way to forgive,
but stop anyway. Don't transmit
your childhood — the axe through the TV
when you were watching Saturday morning cartoons,
and when you cried, the fists to your face.

One day his heart will break
over what he's about to do. But today
he twists the green meat of a thick branch
until it snaps, strips the fresh bark

with his pocket knife like a hunter,
his heart and mind untouchable,
certain of the correction necessary.
Back inside, he rams the bathroom door,
the hook popping. He yanks open
the shower curtain, revealing the boy
who can't tell what weapon of choice
the intruder holds dark and blurry.

I want to get in between the blind,
surprised boy, the screw-up who's trying
to be his father, and take the hits.
The man's shouting gibberish, the boy's
trying to protect his dick, the switch
landing on his arms, chest, thighs,
stomach, shoulders, hard enough to sting
but bruise minimally. The man's got enough control
not to hit his face, his hands, anywhere
those welts like a pox on the heart
can be seen. The way the pain settles
into softer flesh is the man's way of saying
this boy's spoiled life isn't so bad.
He could've gotten the axe.

Oliver Sacks:
A Hero's Journey

by Harvey Blume

ZEITGEIST

On a sunny day in an outdoor cafe in mid-August, I found myself thoroughly absorbed in Oliver Sacks's memoir, *On the Move: A Life*, sometimes laughing out loud at the stories it tells, not that Sacks ever strives for hilarity; it's more that neurology, at least as he practiced and experienced it, can trigger bursts, spasms — Tourettic tics? — of humor.

As I put the book down for a moment, I heard a man at an adjacent table tell his two companions about his history of migraine headaches, and that the best book he had found on the subject was... *Migraine* by Oliver Sacks. By coincidence, I had just then finished the chapter in his memoir Sacks devotes to migraine, and mentioned it to my neighbors. They were well-versed in Sacks, and eager to talk about him, all the more so because they knew that he was dying. Striking as these coffeehouse coincidences seemed to me, I'm sure they were hardly unique. People online and off were talking about Oliver Sacks.

The migraine sufferer reeled off *The Island of the Colorblind* and *Musicophilia: Tales of Music and the Brain* as two of the Sacks books he liked the best, but added that his real favorite was *A Leg to Stand On*. Another coincidence: though not one of Sacks's better-known works, it had also been my favorite, and the occasion for the interview with Sacks that I'm republishing here.

In books like *Awakenings, The Man Who Mistook His Wife for a Hat and Other Clinical Tales*, and *An Anthropologist on Mars: Seven Paradoxical Tales*, Sacks, by bringing neurology to bear on conditions that had been misunderstood or shunted aside, furnished art and literature with new subjects and new kinds of characters. There's Lionel Essrog, for example, the vibrant Tourettic hero of Jonathan Lethem's novel, *Motherless Brooklyn* (1999), and Christopher, the fifteen-year-old autistic boy in Mark Haddon's novel, *The Curious Incident of the Dog in the Night-Time* (2003), which has been adapted into an award-winning Broadway play. It would be very easy to follow these examples up with a host of other stories, novels, studies, and films inspired by the work of Sacks, including, of course, *Awakenings*, the movie based on his book, in which Robert De Niro plays a patient and Robin Williams a neurologist.

TRUCK STOP

From early on, Sacks kept notebooks of his thoughts and experiences, thousands of them. He was always writing, which necessitates a lot of sitting. Yet movement was essential to him.

The title of his memoir comes from a poem by his friend, the poet Thom Gunn, which "instantly resonated" with him in his youth, when, as he puts it, "Most of all, I loved motorbikes." Of his time working at UCLA he writes, "By day I would be the genial, white-coated Dr. Oliver Sacks, but at nightfall I would exchange my white coat for my motorbike leathers and, anonymous, wolf-like, slip out of the hospital. . . then race along the moonlit road."

Midway on one trip back from California to New York City his bike died, and Sacks was picked up by long-distance truckers, staying for a few nights at a truck stop with them. Here's his diary entry about the truck stop:

> Truckers are generally solitary men. Yet occasionally — as in a hot and crowded truckers' cafe, listening to some infinitely familiar record blaring on the jukebox — they are stirred, transfigured suddenly without words or actions, from an inert crowd to a proud community: each man still anonymous and transient, yet knowing his identity with those around him, all those who came before him, and all those who are figured in the songs and ballads.

At an Alabama truck stop, Sacks finds truckers "stirred, transfigured" — Sacksian truckers. Whether in motorcycle leathers or in a medical white coat, whether observing truckers or Postencephalitic patients under his care who, as recounted in Awakenings, were released from their frozen state to flicker, briefly but intensely, back to life, Sacks was irresistibly drawn to transfigurations. Where others might see only deficit, his genius was to find unexpected enhancements. Where others might detail only the particulars of a handicap, he'd show how brains could compensate, and be reshaped and recalibrated, rather than only reduced.

HANDICAPS

Sacks brought his own set of constraints and compensations to his studies, starting with the fact that he was prosopagnosiac, or in plain English, face-blind. He could not recognize people by faces, as most of us do — quickly and from early-on in one's life, where being able to pick mom and dad out of a crowd, for example, is a useful trait for any child to possess. But face-blind folk are not helpless with regard to people-recognition; they rely on visual clues — a beard, say, or hairstyle, height, weight, gait — and on assists from other senses. Sacks writes about an encounter with

Mae West, who had come to his hospital for a minor procedure, that he didn't recognize her face, but "recognized her voice — how could one not?"

And he suffered migraines, which presented him with a question at an early age that went beyond face-recognition, namely, "How did we *recognize* anything?" During a migraine: "My vision could be unmade, deconstructed, frighteningly but fascinatingly, in front of me, and then be remade, reconstructed, all in the space of a few minutes."

Migraine helped drive Sacks to the study of neurology for answers. Migraine became the subject of his first book, though in it he maintains a clinical distance from personal experience. *A Leg to Stand On* collapses the distance, which is why it was his hardest book to write, took years, and went through so many drafts.

The tale starts with Sacks on holiday in Norway, blithely contemplating a hike up a mountain trail. At the base of the trail he noted a sign saying: "Beware of the Bull," which included a cartoon "of a man being tossed by a bull." This "must be the Norwegian sense of humor" he reasoned. "How could you keep a bull on a mountain?"

The Norwegians weren't kidding. There was in fact a big white bull residing atop that Norwegian cliff. At first, it seemed placid and beautiful, but transfiguration works both ways. Remember that scene in *Raiders of the Lost Ark* where the beatific angels swirling out of the opened ark turn into angels of death? That's how it was for Sacks and the bull, as the bull became "hideous — hideous beyond belief, hideous in strength, malevolence and cunning. It seemed now to be stamped with the infernal in every feature. It became, first a monster, and now the Devil." Panicked, sure the bull was right behind him — "I heard heavy, thudding footsteps and heavy breathing behind me" — he plunged down a slippery path and wound up with his left leg "twisted grotesquely underneath me and in my knee such pain as I had never, ever known." He managed to splint his leg with an umbrella he'd luckily brought along, righted himself, and soldiered slowly on, until he couldn't, as it began to get cold and dark and it was all he could do to remain conscious. Then, suddenly, he heard a "long yodeling call," and was discovered by "reindeer hunters, father and son, who had pitched camp nearby." Before long, villagers arrived to carry him to town on a litter.

All that transpires in the first pages of the book. The real adventure is about to begin. Sacks gets the right medical care and the leg mends, except for the maddening detail that it bears no relation to him; he's convinced it's not his leg. No matter what the doctors and nurses tell him, or his eyes report, he remains positive: *"I had lost my leg."* Oh, he's read about, even treated such cases, and has ample medical vocabulary for them — *somatophrenia phantastica*, Pötzl syndrome, scotoma, scotoma for the leg. But now that he is such a case — a patient rather than the sympathetic, learned neurologist he is accustomed to being — such terminology does not suffice, does not keep him from returning in his dreams again and again to his "non-leg." He turns to John Donne and the Psalms for relevant literature. He listens, endlessly, to Mendelssohn's Violin Concerto, a piece of music he had previously considered "trifling" but now gives him the sense of "quickening" he craved. And he thinks about Lurianic Kabbalah.

Lurianic Kabbalah was promulgated by Rabbi Isaac Luria when he settled in Safed (in what's now Israel) after the 1492 Expulsion of the Jews from Spain, where Jews had lived in fairly consistent harmony with Christian and Islamic culture for centuries. For Luria, the Expulsion was a cosmic explosion, a catastrophe not just for Jews but for God, who was splintered, shattered, wounded and badly in need of re-integration.

Like Sacks.

Tempted at first by the idea, Sacks finally rejected giving *A Leg to Stand On* a Kabbalistic armature, and kept seeking a form that would allow him to portray his "own intimate feelings in a way which more 'doctorly' writings had never done." The result is what he dubbed a "neurological novel." Imprecise if not indefinable as that term might be, there is no doubt that the book adheres to the arc of much great narrative — innocence and ignorance; descent, pain, unraveling, decomposition; and finally, recomposition and return.

In other words, the hero's journey.

TERRORS

Given his genial persona — bubbly, compassionate, explanatory, consoling — it's easy to underestimate how terrified Sacks could be, and the role of terror in his life, and not only in face of a white bull on a mountain. His older brother Michael was violently psychotic. "Terrified, and deeply embarrassed — how could we invite friends, relatives, colleagues, *anyone*, to the house with Michael raving and rampaging upstairs," Sacks had to leave London to escape Michael. "I felt a passionate sympathy for him, I half-knew what he was going through, but I had to keep a distance also, create my own world of science so that I would not be swept into the chaos, the madness, the seduction, of his."

Sacks has described himself as feeling "very distracted much of the time, darting from one thing to another." In fact, only terrifying extremes seemed to settle him down, concentrate his fractured attention. He often took his motorcycle to 100 mph. He was a regular at Muscle Beach in California, where he set a record for squats (rising up from a crouch with weight on your shoulders), setting a Muscle Beach record of 600 pounds. (That, he writes, is why Mae West invited him to her Malibu mansion though he didn't at first recognize her; she liked having young musclemen around.) He took life-threatening amounts of amphetamine.

He quit the amphetamines only when he knew he would write a book, *Migraine*, which he did, and from then on devote himself to an "oeuvre."

OEUVRE

Sacks never propagandized for neurology as opposed to psychology, and, significantly, never polemicized against Freud. It was simply not his style, as it was Freud's, to polemicize for and defend an overarching, ever-expanding theoretical superstructure, a master narrative. Sacks, in fact, admired Freud immensely, for years kept a copy of *The Interpretation of Dreams* with him, and was in psychoanalysis for decades — although, as he remarks in *On The Move*, there were times when he failed to recognize the therapist he had been seeing twice weekly for years. "This failure to recognize him came up as a topic . . . I think that he did not entirely believe me when I maintained that it had a neurological basis rather than a psychiatric one."

Though Sacks recounts it casually, off-handedly, the incident is telling. No one more than Sacks has disrupted what Auden termed the "whole climate of opinion" that had collected, if not coagulated, around Freud.

Freud fixated on the "unrememberable and unforgettable" events of childhood, which for him were the mysteries at the roots of our being. (That they were "unrememberable and unforgettable" gave him enviable license for defining and redefining them as he saw fit.) Sacks, on the other hand, proposed — to his therapist, and by means of his writings to the culture at large — that if we have a genuine appetite for mystery, we might do well to think about those of the brain.

Sacks's friend Stephen Jay Gould put it well about the Freud v. Sacks dichotomy, taking note of the fact that Sacks had in his youth been an avid motorcyclist and an always-keen naturalist.

For Sacks's sixty-fourth birthday Gould wrote:

> This man, who's in love with a cycad
> But once could have starred in a bike ad
> King of multidiversity
> Hip! Happy birth-i-day
> You exceed what old Freud, past head psych, had.

The Freudian climate has dissipated. If there's anything comparable today, Sacks is near its center, with Sacks, not Freud, the master-narrator. You might say, oh, well, the study of mind goes through fashions and has its seasons. But you also might recognize that there is such a thing as progress.

LOSS

Sacks is gone. When the news came that he had died on August 30 of the terminal cancer he learned he had in February, I felt it personally, as did I'm sure many others, including my friends at the outdoor coffeehouse. To quote another friend: we woke to "a sad morning without Dr. Sacks." But I wouldn't be completely honest if I didn't add that along with the sadness I felt a twinge of envy as I read through *On The Move*. What a life: what an utterly amazing — amazingly expressed, amazingly useful — life this Oliver Sacks lived.

INTERVIEW

[In 1995, Harvey Blume interviewed Oliver Sacks for an article in the Boston Book Review, "The Casebook of Oliver Sacks," where Sacks discussed in detail his books, his career, his devotion to neurology, and a wide range of other topics. We republish it here.]

"We are in strange waters here, where all the usual considerations may be reversed — where illness may be wellness, and normality illness, where excitement may be either bondage or release...It is the very realm of Cupid and Dionysus."

from *The Man Who Mistook His Wife for a Hat*

Oliver Sacks: People ask, are you still a doctor, do you still see patients, or are you just a writer? As you just saw for yourself [a man in a wheelchair had just left the hotel room where we talked] I see patients. It is my life and I never want to stop.

Harvey Blume: In *A Leg to Stand On*, you write, "If my attention is engaged, I cannot disengage it...It makes me an investigator. It makes me an obsessional. It makes me, in this case, an explorer of the abyss..." Do you have a neurological disorder that compels you to examine neurological disorders?

OS: I feel very distracted much of the time, darting from one thing to another but I think there is some sort of consistency or tenacity to it.

HB: And in *An Anthropologist on Mars* you describe yourself as a physician called "to make house calls, house calls at the far borders of human experience." That would seem to apply to all your work.

OS: This man in the wheelchair was a house call. It was exactly what my father would have done when I was a kid. I used to love to go with my father on house calls. He was often called a whiz at diagnosis. It got around and if he went to Edinburgh or Lisbon someone would know and phone him up. He would see them in his hotel room.

HB: So you carry on the tradition. But I hope you won't be offended if I say that your work brings to mind P.T. Barnum and the age-old fascination with borderline human experiences.

OS: I think it does, although I'm obviously vulnerable and sensitive to the notion of Sacks's freak show. Museums started partly as cabinets of curiosities — wonders, marvels, and prodigies.

HB: The boundary conditions of being human have always been of interest.

OS: For me it's a way of looking at being human rather than being inhuman.

When I was young my mother, who was a surgeon, used to take me to the Royal College of Surgeons Museum. That was Hunter's original 18th century museum. It still had a skeleton of the Irish giant, the Sicilian dwarf and the skulls of Turgenev and Anatole France next to each other. And my father would tell me, when he had been a young man at the London hospital the Elephant Man was still a memory for many people. So if you want, looking for prodigiousness is in me but always to illustrate the extent of humanity, of human capacity and diversity.

I was very moved some years ago in a Mennonite village in northern Canada where a fifth of the population has Tourette's. I was wondering how this deeply religious community would deal with it. Basically, their attitude was similar to that expressed in an old Jewish blessing to be said on seeing a strange person: you praise God for the diversity of Creation.

HB: In *A Leg to Stand On*, which is about your own accident and recovery, you describe turning to the Psalms at a certain point; you describe the Psalms as case histories. This applies, in reverse, to your own work. You turn your case histories into psalms; you look for the redemptive value in people's experience of suffering and anomaly.

OS: Somewhere I quote Nietzsche from the preface to *The Gay Science* where he says suffering doesn't make us better but it may make us more profound; it makes us descend into our depths; it makes one question more severely than one has questioned before.

I am certainly very conscious of this deepening and pensive quality, this reflective quality in many patients. There are also those who are destroyed — devastated, embittered, maddened. But there are those who are strengthened, who discover other resources, and who are transformed in some sort of way, physiologically and neurologically. But I certainly would not, as it were, prescribe an affliction for its redemptive power.

HB: Though in *A Leg to Stand On* there is a sense in which you feel privileged to have undergone that journey.

OS: I think I did, and this is partly what A.R. Luria [a Russian neurologist] said to me when I wrote to him — and he is, in a way, my mentor, both spiritual and neurological. He said, I'm sorry this happened to you but since it did, since you have this power of introspection and articulation, describe it from the inside as it's never been described before. That is what I tried to do. But some of the other patients in hospital said to me, you lucky bugger, we're suffering and you're turning it into a book.

HB: *A Leg to Stand On* is a story of descent, a literal descent down a hill and a descent into the self. You look into the face of a bull near the top of the hill. The bull doesn't do anything; he doesn't chase you.

OS: No, no he was probably sitting there placidly.

HB: And all of a sudden you see the devil. You flee and severely injure yourself.

OS: I found that the most difficult of all books, partly because every time I worked on it I would be thrown back into an unbearable reliving of the situation.

HB: One minute it's *The Sound of Music* — there you are, striding confidently uphill — and then it's suddenly The Cabinet of Dr. Caligari where everything is dark, grotesque, disassociated, fragmentary.

OS: I was haunted by this experience. I was in danger of having it again if I couldn't get it out.

I suggest half-facetiously that the book should be read under spinal anesthesia so the reader will know in himself what I'm talking about. These things are really quite unimaginable. When you have it, you cannot imagine it otherwise, and when it's not there you can't imagine it. The absolute unimaginability of all sorts of terrible neural knowledge which comes and goes is what I'm talking about.

A very Parkinsonian patient of mine managed, before he froze up, to inject himself with medication. A minute later he straightened and said, "I have forgotten how to be Parkinsonian." Then he added, "In forty or fifty minutes, when it wears off, the terrible knowledge of how to be Parkinsonian will come back."

HB: *A Leg to Stand On* is a portrayal of a nightmare, a story of being lost in one's alienation.

OS: This particular sort of nightmare, alienation from one's limbs, is extremely difficult, first of all, for the person to communicate to the doctor. But if a communication can be made, it is then very difficult for the doctor to communicate it further.

William Mitchell, the first to describe phantom limbs, originally used a fictional form. But the negative phantom — the absence, the alienation — has never made its way very well into the medical literature.

HB: Though it's the kind of thing 20th century literature is so good at portraying.

OS: And it existed under Hippocrates.

HB: You describe *A Leg to Stand On* as a neurological novel. In what sense is it a novel?

OS: I don't know. Actually, I'm not a novel reader or writer and I'm no good at plot design and character; I'm a chronicler. Genre is not a word I use a lot. I don't know what is meant by deconstruction. I'm ignorant of literary theory and indifferent to it. I don't think of myself as a writer or an artist. Well, I do and I don't.

HB: In *Awakenings* you prescribe art as a remedy for your patients. Art seems central to your work.

OS: At all sorts of levels, including the level of the man I just saw, who often can't walk but he can dance. Certainly the case history itself has to be almost equally art and science.

I don't know who my models are. Like many people of my generation, I adored the H. G. Wells short stories and was also very fond of Chesterton. I footnote Wells's "Country of the Blind," though strangely that footnote has only become relevant in an experience I've had subsequently, when, last summer, I went to an island of the colorblind and saw a whole community who for two centuries have had no perception and no conception of color. They've organized their lives in completely different terms and regard us so-called color normals as distracted by chromatic hallucinations.

My tastes are rather conventional. I was brought up with Dickens and Trollope. My mother used to read D.H. Lawrence stories to me when I was young. I just came across a marvelous poem of D.H. Lawrence in which he speaks of how red is essentially sensuous and how "even God can't think of red."

Writers who may have been a model for me — I still love reading them — are the naturalists. I love Humboldt's personal narratives, Darwin on the Beagle, Wallace in Malaya, the notion of the scientific adventure. For that matter, I'm fond of Conan Doyle, not only Sherlock Holmes but the Challenger books, especially *The Lost World*. I used to know it by heart.

HB: You talk about Sherlock Holmes as possibly an autistic personality. It's also tempting to think of you as a Sherlock Holmes type setting out to unravel mysteries.

OS: It's not clear that Holmes's cases form an oeuvre, that there's a movement, that they're connected one with the other, that he becomes wiser, that he develops in any way. And I hope for something like that. I do feel called to a case here and a case there and I like being on the case but I do hope at a deeper level, which Holmes doesn't have, there's something happening.

HB: Doyle sends Holmes off to demystify the world, to solve all mysteries and leave none intact. And then, of course, Doyle himself becomes a spiritualist.

OS: I'm very much, myself, for mystery. I'm very much against mysticism. I feel for example that Stephen Wiltshire, in *An Anthropologist on Mars*, is quite mysterious; I don't know what goes on in him. I don't know that I mean mysterious like the Trinity, which is merely incomprehensible. I don't understand mystery in that sense. But it may be mysterious like late Beethoven.

HB: Dreams play a crucial role in so much of your work.

OS: I have published a paper called "Neurological Dreams" which examines the level at which neurological events enter dreams. For example, I describe such a dream in *A Leg to Stand On* where there's an annihilation bomb that is a migraine entering the dream. I also approached this in "The Last Hippie." Physiologically, one sees there's less and less difference, in some ways, between the waking and the dreaming state, and there's the notion that waking is, in fact, dreaming in the world; it's dreaming within the constraints of external perception. So I do think of dreaming as almost the most fundamental mode of being a human being. I have sometimes said that I think of Tourette's as a form of public dreaming, in which outer events and inner events join in manifest dreaming, visible and audible.

I don't believe in prognostication in any deep sense, although I think that work may be done in dreams which may alter reality. I give an example of that in *A Leg to Stand On* when I was asked to put down a crutch and walk. I tried and fell over. Then I had a dream in which I threw the crutch away. I woke up and immediately did so; it had been rehearsed in the dream. Why or how Magda, in *Awakenings*, dreamed she was going to die the day she did, I don't know.

I go along with Freud about the occult; I'm very fond of mystery; I hate the occult.

HB: You have a romantic notion that the distinction between illness and health is blurred, and that illness can be not a deficit but an enhancement, as in Thomas Mann's *Dr. Faustus*.

OS: Indeed, I quote it at length in the "Leg" book.

HB: In *The Man Who Mistook His Wife for a Hat* you wrote, "What a paradox, what a cruelty…that inner life and imagination may lie dull and dormant, unless released, awakened, by an intoxication or disease!"

OS: Yes, that was about Natasha, who said I feel so well I must be ill.

And I think of that last novella of Thomas Mann, *The Black Swan*, where a post-menopausal woman at a spa feeling fortyish and sad meets a young man who's very attentive. She falls in love and starts to feel marvelous. Then, strangely, she bleeds again. Perhaps her periods are coming back, her youth returning. Everyone compliments her. Then she starts to feel ill and gets a bad color and has a huge hemorrhage. In the last scene, she is on the operating table. The surgeons are talking. She has a secreting tumor in her ovary, which has metastasized everywhere. One of them says, something like this would produce a great surge of estrogen, of hormones, and might produce an aphrodisiac state. Another says, perhaps it's the other way around; perhaps falling in love can cause the ovarian tumor.

Certainly with something like Tourette's, whatever the suffering and disability, there may also be energy and spontaneity. I was just in Toronto seeing a friend of mine, a very Tourettic artist. Sometimes the Tourette's can tear him apart; it can be full of a pantomimic impulse. Other times it can all rush together in the form of creativity. He doesn't want medication because he fears it will take the edge off, although when I see how terrifying it is I fear for him.

People have called me on romanticizing illness and there may be some truth to it; I'm prepared to retract that somewhat. But what interests me, especially now, is that new health is to be achieved through reorganizing. So that in the case of the colorblind artist, he first of all finds himself in an impoverished, ugly, abnormal world drained of meaning and feeling because color had been such a vehicle for him. At that point he is suicidal; he feels it's the end of him and his art. Then, the change occurs. What had been hideous and ugly and impoverished becomes fascinating, privileged and beautiful.

HB: So the implication may be not, say, that Beethoven only coped well with silence but perhaps that he learned from silence, heard something new in it.

OS: Perhaps became a different sort of composer. I thought of this most deeply in regard to the colorblind artist, who clearly went through a descent and a redemption but the redemption was to a different form of being, into a quite different life of art and the imagination. It's one of the clearest examples for me of loss in one way, and redemption through reorganization.

HB: At the end of the piece on Stephen Wiltshire in *An Anthropologist on Mars*, you ask, "Was not art, quintessentially, an expression of a personal vision, a self? Could one be an artist without having a 'self'?" Are you prepared to answer that question?

OS: No. That's why I left it as a question. The whole book is full of questions. I'm an inquirer more than an answerer.

Reporter's Notebook: Inside the Brothels of Mumbai

by Shanoor Seervai

I am seated cross-legged on a brothel floor on a hot April afternoon. The door is ajar. Just beyond it, a disheveled man in a grey pinstriped shirt appears at the top of the dank staircase, ducking to avoid banging his head on the low ceiling. The hinges creak as he slips in.

"Is Lata here?" he asks.

"Lata has gone back to the village," says Roshni, a chatty woman with bulging hips who, now in her thirties, has risen up the ranks to become the keeper of this three-room affair. "But you can sit with Payal if you like."

To sit, *baithna* in Hindi, is a euphemism sex workers use.

The man looks at Payal, plopped on a bamboo mat on the floor beside me, the ringlets in her hair escaping from a loose bun. He hesitates. Payal remains silent, expressionless, tuned to the 14-inch TV on the wall rather than the prospective customer.

His eyes flit from her to me. He shakes his head no and slinks back down the stairs.

My obviously alien presence embarrassed him, I know. He was squeamish about buying sex while an outsider watched.

I'm torn between satisfaction my interview wasn't interrupted and guilt over depriving Payal of rare afternoon business. I am no longer naïve enough to believe I've saved her from the indignity of selling her body.

Roshni resumes narrating the story of how she ended up in Mumbai. The burn scars on her upper arms mark when her husband doused her with a pot of boiling mutton stew. Roshni demonstrates how she had been curled up at the time, "with my legs like this, held against my chest," she says. "It's a good thing or I would have gotten completely burned. I'd just had an operation to stop myself from having babies."

Roshni left home that day with her two young children. For hours she walked along a country road because she couldn't bear the humiliation of sitting on a bus reeking of mutton stew.

At her parents' house, the husband of Roshni's older sister tried to sleep with her. She left and found a job as a maid at a hotel. The owner tried to take advantage of her. She accepted a woman's offer to work at a cotton shop in Mumbai. It turned out to be a brothel. But by the time she realized she'd been tricked, it was too late. Roshni had children to feed, whether by working loom or loins.

Roshni's story is hardly unique. In dozens of interviews with sex workers and their children, almost all have told me stories of absent men — usually dead fathers or drunk, abusive husbands — illiteracy, and no decent jobs. In addition to their own sustenance, a great many are responsible for their elderly parents, daughters, and sons.

These tales are brutal, but from each I try to glean insights that might help me diagnose why sex work is so rampant and devastating in India.

Besides the mental strain, reporting from Kamathipura poses another challenge. I am an outsider. I must be careful. When I visited the brothels as a college student, the field workers of the NGO I volunteered with never left me alone. A young woman, fair and tall, they told me, would attract curious and lewd stares from pimps and johns. They sought to avoid trouble.

When I decided to return to Kamathipura more recently as a reporter, I still didn't feel comfortable walking around the area and going into the brothels completely alone. I came to an arrangement with a community organization in the red-light district, a federation of sex workers called Asha Darpan. They allow me to come to their office — a hole in the wall sandwiched between a shoe-repair store and a vendor of fried snacks — and I accompany the staff to brothels for health check-ups and to distribute condoms. I tell them where I will be and am free to speak with whomever I want. They pick me up when it's time to leave.

From noon to 7 p.m. — when *dhandha,* or sex work, is slowest — I do my reporting, armed with a notebook and recorder, dressed in my baggy, washed-out salwaar khameezes. Sometimes the sex workers running the organization interrogate me for a while first. They are understandably perplexed by my endeavor. My home, an eight-minute train ride from theirs, is as foreign as another planet. It can be exasperating trying to explain what the heck I am doing here.

Roshni, at the end of our interview, asks the usual dreaded questions. Why are you writing all this down? What are you going to get out of it? I stumble to convey how I desire to be the sort of reporter who doesn't just chase the news but tells the stories of people without a voice, without recourse.

But Sailesh, a transgender sex worker and peer counselor at Asha Darpan who has come to collect me at the end of my visit, cuts me off.

"See, you and me," he says to Roshni, "we're from this line."

What line? I wonder.

"She," Sailesh motions to me with his chin, "is from the family line."

"People in the family line, they think sex workers only do *dhandha*. But there's much more to our lives — we have homes, we cook food, we have children. She wants to see what that is. She writes it down so she can tell other people in the family line that, actually, this is what sex workers do."

The family line. I never thought about it that way before. But the phrase makes sense in the context of a group that feels shunned by India's intractable notions of family values and rigid morality. I belong to a different "line," not only because of socioeconomics but because of my ability to have familial relationships instead of transactional ones, *dhandha*.

I Want To Tell You Something

by Susan Volchok

*W*as it your farting woke me? The next sound I hear is such a percussive, protracted arse bleat, and the stink of it hangs so heavy and sour over the bed, I decide you probably have trumpeted me awake. Blow, Gabriel, blow! But it's a grim thought; I'm in no mood even for my own humor. Of course, you've thrown all the covers over me as well, so that you might fart freely and with full abandon into the already stale midnight air of the bedroom, so that I'm drenched in sweat, utterly tangled in a heavy twist of sheets and quilt. It may actually have been this that woke me first. Or some combination of these assaults on my senses, my sense of order. I sit up, nostrils shriveling, nerves aquiver with a still mild indignation.

I set myself to refolding and arranging, turning the bedclothes down until just our feet are covered, pulling the cool sheet back up over both our bodies. These methodical movements calm me. The fluorescent digits of the clock radio read one-thirteen a.m. I've been asleep less than an hour. I stretch out on my left side with my back to you and close my eyes, trying to find my way again into dreams.

You thrust the bedding off yourself with a violent kick, shoving the bulky mess onto my side of the bed, pinning it there with the full dead weight of your leg. You let fly another outrageous brrraaap.

"Pig. You disgusting pig," I mutter. The obvious animal. Poor things, I know they don't deserve the comparison. But I'm so tired, at a loss for more precise words. I fling myself into action again, whipping things back into place, into an approximation of my previous arrangement. You startle, somewhere down there in your own peaceful dreamland.

"Huh?" you sigh. "Huh?" That's it – your response verbatim. You're asleep, after all. Yet somehow, you manage to hook your foot around the edge of the covers. I pull them away: "Stop it, just stop it," I hiss. I restore them to their recent orderliness. I lie down, close my eyes, only to realize that I'm not merely awake, having been awakened. I am absolutely, stark wide-awake. I'm going to have trouble now; I'm not going to be able to just drift back into sleep.

And you've begun to snore. Not, admittedly, the stentorian snoring of which you're capable when sprawled out on your back. No, these are the stupid little puttputt sounds you sometimes make, mouth breathing in a sideways position. I realize with horror that I can actually transcribe this new refrain, its pattern subtle but certain: Poopah (ph ph)…poopah (ph ph). This isn't all. Every so often, you stop the popping just long enough to scratch some part of your body. Compulsive, noisy. It's only your own hairy chest, belly, balls. Yet it's as unspeakable as fingernails screeched across a blackboard.

I turn toward you, glaring, half-hoping a baleful look will be enough to wake you, though I'm not certain what I would say. Even in the midst of my rising outrage, I have a dim sense of overreacting, of being irrationally wrought up. I am watching myself watch you, and it is not a pretty sight. I'm reminded of the macabre Japanese short story I've just read, about a woman who has ceased to sleep, and the ways in which her view of her husband (who of course goes on sleeping and waking and living his normal life) becomes more and more grotesque, unto real repulsion and loathing, although she's always assured herself theirs is a happy marriage.

Another ferocious fart. This prodigious windy production reeks of a whole day's badly digested bad food. (You ate no meals at home today, you won't mind my pointing out, not even taking time for the usual toaster oven waffles at breakfast this morning).

"Pig!" I say, right out loud.

I give you a good shove with my knee. You moan, roll onto your back, legs dragging at the bedding, which falls with a soft thud to the floor; your mouth falls open, and you begin to snore in earnest. Your chest heaves; your sinuses resonate. I leap out of bed, haul the bedclothes back up onto the foot of the mattress, then leave them in disarray and retreat to the bathroom, slamming the door after me. I don't even turn on the light, I just sit down on the lidded toilet seat, clenching my fists, cursing you with what sound like powerful curses, but are too conventional to do any real good. You fucking, farting asshole; you snoring shit; I wish I could fart right in your face; I could strangle you in your sleep, you animal….

I genuinely believe I could throttle you to death. I could. Yet here I remain, sitting alone on the toilet in our little bathroom with the door shut between us, rather than shaking or shouting you awake to tell you exactly how wretched your flatulence and flinging and snoring and ass scratching make me feel.

When I do finally venture out, all is calm and still in the bedroom. The whiff of your night work remains in the air, but it isn't gut wrenching, galvanizing. And the room is silent. I stop at the foot of the bed, seize two corners of the bedding, and struggle alone one more time to smooth and straighten everything across this double mattress we've shared for sixteen years. I slide between the sheets, on my back with my eyes closed, arms at my sides. Like a corpse in a coffin, or maybe like an anxious new bride – something, anyway, other than a longtime lover and life companion.

How much like an old dog you are. Lying there completely oblivious, your body doing whatever it wants to, unconcerned with anything but your own comfort. If you really were that old dog, my own old dog, I would just hold my nose against your stink, maybe even laugh a little. I wouldn't mind your growling in your sleep, your fitful scratching; I might even be comforted by these things, because they would mean you were here to protect me and love me and keep me company. I would reach out my hand from time to time to pet you, rubbing my palm the wrong way along your wiry hair; you would groan, down to the depths of your doggy sleep, pure pleasure at my touch. I wonder why I should feel so much more tenderness toward the disgusting old dog I've never owned and will probably never own, than toward a man with whom I have lived for so long.

I drift for a few hours. When I wake, the clock reads four fifteen, and our youngest is shifting and sighing in the next room. The ensuing silence reassures me she is still asleep. I'm ridiculously relieved, and smile at the thought of the catchphrase with which she prefaces nearly everything she says. "I want to tell you something." It's what she would have said if she had padded in here to stand over me, waiting for my eyes to snap open.

I want to tell you something. It doesn't necessarily signify that she has a whole story to tell; this is how she begins whatever it is she's bent on telling. It expresses an intention, announces that she will now say something she considers significant, worth saying. Above all, it means to get your attention.

I want to tell you something. In the middle of the night. I wish I knew what it was. She doesn't always know what it is either.

That's the real purpose of her pat phrase, I suppose, to bridge the unbearable distance between silence and speech. I want to tell you something.

Without warning, you roll toward me with a mulish kick at the covers, a full throated moan, a noiselessly escaping exhalation from beneath. SBDs, silent but deadly, kids used to call them in school. I pull myself up on my elbows, look into your face. It is still entirely asleep. It doesn't know, doesn't see or hear. Your forehead glistens with perspiration. Maybe a bad dream. Maybe you're not feeling well. Or maybe it's nothing at all. I pass my palm lightly across the sweating expanse of skin. Your eyes flicker open for an instant, fix on mine; you smile. "Mmm," you say dreamily. Pure pleasure at my touch. I smile too. Your eyes close again; you turn away. I turn so that we're back to back as we were at the beginning, almost, but not quite touching one another. Then, I draw the sheet up over my hip, tuck a corner beneath my armpit, taut over one breast, and close my eyes, waiting for the sounds of a radio orchestra to wake me next.

The truth of low-hanging clouds

by Jonathan Weinert

Tiepolesque: is that a word? If not, it should be:
all these clouds stacked up and shadowed blue,
as if the gods had finally deigned to reappear.

It's easy to imagine them streaming
from the cumuli: that one's gilt winged shoes and fillet,
this one's blinding chiton; that one's hair

a few shades blonder than a stook of wheat,
this one's black as charcoaled timbers.
I admit I find their pluperfect bodies—

the geometrical precision of their thighs,
the killer abs, the cheekbones sharp enough

to butcher meat—a little . . . vulgar. Next to them,
my frame seems rough-cut, badly finished.
Whoever colored me didn't stay within the lines.

I see this through the window of a Starbucks,
understand, but why shouldn't there be
another Renaissance, a looking back

that also serves to purge this moment
of its willful superstitions, such as personhood?
Who *doesn't* need her vision to include

ungovernable forces: the city on the hill
as well as the tempest that destroys it,

the pretty seaside home as well as
the freak wave that scrapes it clean away?
The wave, which smells of hake and Cherry Coke,

slides back, and up and down the seaboard
come reports of strange things flying in the air.
If I could call to them, I would, but then

that's always been a gamble. I don't know
what furies what I say may summon. The sun
strikes crowns of rays from denim weathers.

One day it all comes true, depending on
what "it" turns out to mean.

The Pervert

by Dwight Livingstone Curtis

1.

The pervert came to Independence on Labor Day, the day before school started. Independence is our street, where we all live. Upper and Lower Independence, but mainly Upper Independence, above the intersection and the gravestone store and the witch's house.

Labor Day was when we got the news, at least. For all we know, he could have been living there already.

We were in Paul Ciofani's basement, drinking IBC root beer and pretending we were drunk. Our parents were upstairs, in the backyard, drinking white wine, red wine, and Heineken.

Paul's basement had a pool table, and a dartboard with a cork wall behind it. There was a NordicTrack machine and an arcade machine. The game was Gradius, and it took quarters. On a shelf behind the machine there was a pickle jar full of them. We asked what happened to the quarters after you fed them into the machine, and Paul said his dad had a way of getting them out. There was always someone playing Gradius when we were in Paul's basement.

What we noticed first were the sounds of footsteps. It was our parents coming inside and standing together in the living room. Some of us went and got our sneakers and packed up our video games and Nerf guns. But no one came downstairs, and when we looked out the window we saw the Parkers' car on the street in front of the house. Ryan Parker had been the oldest kid in the neighborhood before he went away to college, and whenever he was home he set out his street hockey nets for us to play on.

Mr. and Mrs. Parker stayed for an hour. No one came downstairs to get us, and it got dark, and we listened as, one by one, the dads raised their voices.

2.

The pervert had come to the Parkers'. He came to tell them that he was a pervert, and he was going to come to every house on Independence, one by one, to tell us all the same thing. He weighed three hundred pounds. He wore glasses. We imagined that they were smudged, wire-rimmed glasses, like the ones our music teacher wore. We tried to imagine what three hundred pounds looked like. Like Josef, someone said, and we laughed.

Our parents set new rules for us. We compared them on the walk to school. Paul Ciofani wasn't allowed past the intersection, on foot or by bicycle. Sofia Winston's dad had given her a can of Mace, which she kept in her backpack. She took it out and showed it to us. Peter Wiley's mom had told him no more hiding games: no Capture-the-flag, Olly- olly-incomfree, Spud, or Sardines. If the pervert comes around, Paul said, I'd rather be hiding. Yeon Woo's parents hadn't told him anything at all, and he walked in silence, cleaning his glasses on his shirt.

"Does he have to visit when someone's home?" Sofia asked before we went into the school.

How many of our parents were home during the day? Had he already been to our houses, and stood on our porches ringing the bell? Would he have looked through the mail slot to see if anyone was coming? Had he looked for our hidden keys? We knew where all of them were. Peter's was underneath the doormat. Sofia's was in a plastic rock. Paul Ciofani's was underneath a piece of slate on his walk, but we used the back door, which was never locked. Mine was on a string on a nail just inside the mail slot. I could just reach it. I wondered whether three-hundred-pound fingers could fit through the slot.

3.

On Upper Independence, between the cross streets, our houses were connected by backyards. Our street had no government lines on it, just the chalk midline, which we redrew every summer from one intersection to the other. On school nights we played whatever we had enough people for. When the kids from the Townhouses and Lower Independence showed up, we usually played basketball.

There were hoops in front of Paul's house and Peter's house. The rim on Paul's hoop was bent from when a snowplow ran over it, but it was at the dead center of the block, and that's where we were playing on the first Friday after school started, when Roman rode up the street with Josef on his pegs.

Roman was one of the Russians from the Townhouses. He'd been here for two years. His English had gotten worse and worse, and he barely spoke anymore. He lifted weights with the other Russians from the Townhouses. They'd brought dumbbells out to one of the outdoor wooden fitness areas that the town had built, each with a little placard describing the exercises you were supposed to do there. The fitter Roman got, the less basketball he played, and now when he came by he usually just sat on the lawn next to his bike, in a black t-shirt and jeans, and watched the rest of us play. He was in ESL classes, which had the same after-school schedule as Special Ed.

Josef sat on the steps and changed into a pair of sneakers he'd brought in a backpack. They were purple and yellow, and he cinched up the laces but didn't tie them. He tucked the ends back into the ankle of the shoe and pulled his socks up to his knees.

Josef spat when he spoke. He smelled, and he was hairy, and a little older, we guessed, than the rest of us.

"Josef," Paul said. "Are you wearing perfume?"

"It's cologne, you pervert," Josef said. Then he grabbed the ball out of Paul's hands and dribbled it into the street. He was a bad dribbler and his head waggled on his neck. We could see his feet sliding up and down inside his sneakers. He took a shot and missed, and no one went for the rebound.

Josef got mad easily, and when he got mad he eventually cried. He lived on Lower Independence, past the witch's house, and usually had something to do after school, either synagogue, or tutoring, or walking his sister somewhere.

He hung out with kids from the Townhouses. They were immigrants: Koreans and Israelis who stayed for two years, Russians and Germans who stayed for one. We cut through the Townhouses to get to CVS, and we went there for the yard sales on Sundays. The other reason we went to the Townhouses was to look at cars for sale.

It was only my mom, really, who bought them. Our last three cars had come from there. A year ago, my mom and Paul Ciofani and I had biked into the Townhouses and down the main street, looking for signs in the windows. It was the first time I'd been inside a Townhouse, other than when we helped Yeon Woo move to Independence.

It was an Arab family, and only the father spoke English. There were grocery bags stacked everywhere, and huge suitcases open on the living room floor. While my mom spoke with the father, Paul and I looked around the first floor. In the dining room, and in every Townhouse I've been in since, there were cases and cases of bottled water. Even Yeon Woo's family still drank out of a big Poland Spring bubbler in the corner of their dining room.

All Townhouses look the same: there's a kitchen and living room downstairs, and two or three bedrooms and a bathroom upstairs. While we were looking around the house, a little boy came running down the stairwell into the kitchen, sobbing. There was blood seeping out from between his clenched fingers. The father spoke to him and pried open his hand. There was a deep cut across his palm. The father got out a bottle of rubbing alcohol and was about to pour it over the cut when my mother stepped forward and stopped him. After we bought the car, when we were driving back to Upper Independence with our bikes in the back, she said, "It's like they're still living in the Stone Age."

It was just me and her in the house most of the time. My brother Morgan went to boarding school. My mother's bedroom was upstairs and I spent most of my time downstairs. Once, when I got two B-minuses at midterms, she'd told me, "it's your life to fuck up." When Morgan was home, he liked to joke that she was retired from parenting.

Once in a while Josef's dad would drive by. He drove a red Corvette convertible, and he'd leave it idling in the middle of the street. He'd talk to us out the window, and then he'd get out and take a few shots. He always wore white tank tops tucked into blue jeans and a leather jacket.

Josef shot with both hands, and always faded away on one foot, as though he were shooting at the buzzer. Josef's dad shot normally, and we'd keep giving the ball back to him until a car turned onto the street and he had to pull forward or until he ran up and dunked it, signaling that he was done. We kept the hoop at the lowest setting, so that we could dunk. After he dunked he would call Josef over to his car and they'd talk for a few minutes in another language and then Josef's dad would drive away, past the intersection and down Lower Independence to their driveway, where the street just started to slope downward. He always honked twice when he left. A little while later, Josef would pack up his sneakers and leave to eat dinner with his family, though he tried to keep it a secret.

Josef shot for a while and then we played Twenty-one and then Roman got up and took a couple of jerky shots, tucking in his shirt again after each one.

4.

It was a word we were still feeling our way around. All week, we tried it out in new situations. Josef was a pervert because of the way Paul said his fingers smelled after Josef fouled him in the face during a game of Twenty-one. "That's pussy," Josef told us. Later, Paul said it had smelled more like poop.

Paul's Labradoodle Dennis was a pervert for getting a red rocket when Sofia scratched his stomach on the stoop. Roman wasn't really a pervert for the way he dressed or talked about girls or porn, because that was normal for the Russians from the Townhouses. Peter, on the other hand, was a pervert for liking Sofia. He was the one who had started calling her Sofia again. The older kids had all called her Little Sweet. Her brother had been Big Sweet. Peter and Sofia talked on the phone at night, and we could hear the phones ringing when they called each other.

Ezra and Rachel, the two fully retarded kids at school, were both perverts as well. Ezra was a pervert because he dropped his pants and underwear all the way down to his ankles when he peed at the urinal. If you got caught peeing next to him, or even just coming out of the bathroom when he was in there, you were a pervert too.

We liked Ezra, but we hated Rachel. We could hear her barking from our classroom, and shouting "Fuck!" until the school officer came to get her. Other times she would cover her ears and scream until she puked, and then she would have a seizure. What made her a pervert was that she liked to stick her hands down her underwear in class, according to Josef, who spent half his day in Special Ed, and that she had once flashed her chest at a whole bathroom full of boys. Her nipples, they told us, were dark and hard-looking, like the caps of acorns.

In the short conversation we'd had on the walk home from Paul Ciofani's barbeque that first night, my mother had said, "You should know that there's a sex offender who moved into a house nearby." After a few seconds she added, "Apparently he's very fat. If you see him, don't speak to him and come right home."

"Why?" I'd asked, juiced up on energy from the party. I was surprised we'd stayed as long as we had. My mother didn't drink alcohol or caffeine after four o'clock and she usually went to bed by eight-thirty. The only person she socialized with was our neighbor, Mrs. Huang, who didn't speak English.

"Because he's dangerous," she said. It was strange to be outside together in the dark, and we walked slowly because of her hip.

5.

We made a map of the houses the pervert had visited so far. Three days after the Parkers, he went to Sofia's neighbors', who were elderly and who had no kids. Then he went to Yeon Woo's, while we were at school. Yeon Woo said that his parents only spoke Korean, which wasn't true, and that he didn't speak Korean himself, which we also knew wasn't true. When we did hear him speak to his parents, it sounded like he was yelling at them, and we were amazed that he could get away with that.

His parents had probably played dumb, he told us, like they always did when they didn't want to speak to a white person. They wouldn't tell him anything about the visit. We could imagine the scene on Yeon Woo's porch, and all three pairs of glasses glinting in the sunlight.

A few days after that he went to Peter's house. Peter's grandmother, who stayed with them one month a year, was the only one home. There was a conversation: that's all he knew. Did Mrs. Wiley know he was a pervert? Was he a pervert for old people, too? Peter went white.

It was an uneven square: two houses on one side of Upper Independence, one on the other, and one, the Parkers', on a cross street, halfway out of our neighborhood toward the nicer houses at the edge of the golf course. Had he come from somewhere else? Was he just passing through?

6.

In the second week of school, we got homework. There weren't enough kids to play anything except Horse and Twenty-one, until Friday, after dinner, when we all came outside. It was muggy and a few houses had put out citronella candles on their front steps, to keep us from getting Tsetse fever. We lingered around the stoops and jumped our scooters over manhole covers. We could hear an ice cream truck on the other side of the Parkway. Eventually someone got us into a ring and started eeny-meenie-miney-moe.

It was getting dark at night again, and we scattered into the half-light. It had been a couple of weeks since we'd been to our favorite hiding spots. Some were grown over, some had been re-landscaped, and some felt darker or smaller than we remembered from the summer. I climbed onto the roof of Yeon Woo's garage and flattened myself against the warm shingles. Over the fence, I watched the branches shake as Sofia climbed the tree in her side yard.

Ten or fifteen of us hid in the trees and side yards and under the porches of the houses along Upper Independence. Someone else was 'it,' someone from a block or two away, and through his eyes we saw our neighborhood as a wild place, honeycombed with secret spaces. We waited and listened for footsteps and for the shrieks of kids up and down the block being discovered by the searchers.

I felt someone walking down the driveway and I flattened myself against the roof. It was a lone searcher, wearing flip-flops. I listened as he crept into the leaves between the wall of the garage and the fence, crunched a few steps in, and peered into the dark corridor. Then he stepped back out onto the gravel of the driveway. Across from me, two backyards away, I watched Sofia lower herself out of the tree and jog quietly around the far side of her house, moving spots.

It was getting close to the end of the game. I craned my neck. There was no motion in any of the yards I was facing, and no sounds of a chase or a discovery. There was a hunt going on. Then I heard it.

I swung from the roof down onto the picket fence and into the corridor between the garage and the fence. I crashed out through the leaves and followed the sound of the voice up the side yard. I slipped around the side of the house into Yeon Woo's front bushes. They were big, hollow bushes, with room to stand inside.

Peter's mom stood in the street. In front of her, lined up on the curb, were the rest of the kids from the game: possibly all of them, which would mean that I had won. Peter's mom had been saying something as I came around the house, but now she was silent. She scanned the group, and turned to face Sofia, who was standing at the end of the group, breathing hard, the sleeves of her t-shirt bunched up around her shoulders.

"Where is my son?" Mrs. Wiley asked. It was true: Peter was

missing from the group. I hadn't won.

"Where the hell is my son?" she asked again, in a raspy voice. She turned down Independence, toward the intersection, and cupped her hands around her mouth. I slipped out of the bush and back into the side yard.

7.

It was evening and a few of us were sitting on Paul's stoop, trying to get the tiny orange bugs to crawl from the bricks onto our hands, when my mother rode by on her bicycle. Everyone else had already been called to dinner. She had her helmet on, the big white one, with the mirror glued to the side. She was wearing her Discman on a lanyard around her neck, and it jingled against her ID card and all of her keys. She had her long denim skirt rubber-banded to her ankles so it wouldn't catch in the chain. Everyone stared at her except me. She had her headphones in, and didn't look up as she rode by and turned into our driveway.

A few minutes later, I heard my name. I said goodbye and walked across the street, past my house, up the steps and through the side yard to the back door of the Huangs' house next door. My mother was already at the table, still wearing her Discman around her neck. Her headphones hung down next to the leg of her chair. She hadn't paused her book-on-tape, and I could hear it faintly talking from the floor.

Mrs. Huang cooked us dinner on nights when my mom worked late. In exchange, my mom helped her with paperwork that she did a few times a year. Mrs. Huang sewed pockets into all my mother's dresses, and every Sunday, after my mom was done reading them, I brought the newspapers over to the Huangs' house. Sometimes I left them between the screen and the side door, and other times Mrs. Huang caught me and made me carry home dishes of food. We always took the two Huang boys, Richard and

Kenneth, with us when I went to the eye doctor.

Richard and Kenny were younger than me and they weren't really a part of the neighborhood. During the time when the rest of us were outside, they had piano lessons, art lessons, and tutoring. They were quiet except when they fought with each other, which was almost every night that I was over there. They fought with weapons, often the long metal shoehorns with the rubber grips that Mrs. Huang kept by the front door, and I'd seen them draw blood. Richard once kicked through the glass in Kenny's bedroom window. They kept posters on the walls of their bedrooms, big pictures of the skeletal, muscular, and vascular systems of the human body, which they moved around to cover the holes in the walls.

Richard, my mother, and I sat at the table and ate white rice with tiny dried fish, thousand-year-old egg soup, and stinky cabbage. Kenny played the piano in the other room. After a while the piano stopped and the piano teacher let himself out the front door. Kenny came into the kitchen and sat with us. Mrs. Huang never sat down while we were eating. She just kept cooking, for some other dinner I assumed she had with Mr. Huang later on.

After dinner my mother and Mrs. Huang sat down in the dining room and put on their reading glasses and spread out papers on the table. Richard and Kenny and I went upstairs to play N64.

8.

The light in our basement came through small windows at the tops of the cement walls. It was almost dark out. I moved along the wall, putting toys into a white pillowcase. These metal shelves in the basement, next to the couch and the video game TV, were where our old toys ended up, and most of them were dusty and broken. There were Happy Meal collectibles and plastic knives and swords and old Nerf guns. I turned over a translucent, peach-colored squirt gun and warm water dripped out the nozzle. I dried it on my pant leg and put it in the pillowcase.

In the boiler room, on a rusty metal workbench, was my chemistry set. It was as I'd left it. I looked inside a plastic water cup, standing among the canisters of chemicals. Whatever I'd mixed together in it had dried a long time ago, leaving a dark ring in the bottom. There were little black pellets peppered across the surface of the workbench, and I touched one with my thumbnail.

I stopped at the top of the stairs, listening for my mother's footsteps, and heard the chunk-whoosh of the upstairs toilet. I closed the basement door behind me and walked through the kitchen and foyer to the end of the living room, where Morgan's bedroom was. It was dark now, and cooler on this side of the house, and I closed Morgan's door behind me. As my eyes adjusted to the room, I noticed all around me the faint whitish-green aura of glow-in-the-dark toys scattered across the bookshelves and stuffed into the clear plastic toy bins at the foot of Morgan's bed. I picked through the bins for the hundredth time, looking for things he wouldn't miss. I rifled through his Pogs and added a few of them to the pillowcase. Finally, after staring at it for a minute, I put his saw-toothed slammer in my pocket. I went into his bathroom. He had two shower radios. I put the old one in the pillowcase.

9.

On Sunday morning, by the time we woke up, there were police barricades at the ends of Upper and Lower Independence. The Winstons had put out their tiki torches, and the Ciofanis had tied balloons to the crooked rim of their basketball hoop. Even the Parkers had propped open their screen door, and set out Ryan's street hockey nets in the open square of the barricaded intersection. Sofia's dad skated by on his roller skis, wearing his helmet and elbow pads, swinging his legs and clacking his long poles against the asphalt like a daddy longlegs. All of the families had moved their cars into their driveways, and we emerged, one by one, onto our pristine street.

The block party lasted all day. By noon the dads were grilling and the moms were walking in a group from lawn to lawn, pointing at flowers and bushes. We played street hockey and Spud and Twenty-one. Although the whole street was blocked off, the party was on Upper Independence. A few families walked up from Lower Independence and from the side streets around us, and in the afternoon a group of Russian families from the Townhouses arrived, shyly, with bowls of cellophaned food. An ice cream truck parked just outside the barricade at the intersection, and its song, which sounded the same volume no matter where we were on the block, inside or outside, gave us the idea to walk to Freezer's.

I took some money from the Velcro wallet we kept in the piano bench. My mom left twenties inside for me to use when I needed them. Sometimes it was empty and I had to remind her, and lately she'd been leaving bigger and bigger amounts for me, less and less often. I always put back my receipts and exact change. The wallet was getting fat with coins, and I kept it hidden under the music books, though I was sure she never checked what was in there. Our house was so empty on days like this that it was scary to be in, wrapped completely in swaying daytime shadows and insulated from the noises of the street. I stayed outside as much as possible, until the last hour before dark, when the other kids got called in for dinner. Mrs. Ciofani or Mrs. Winston always invited me in to eat, but I usually said no. Sundays were a sad night to go to someone else's house. They had chores and homework to do, and people got snappy with each other. Plus, I was embarrassed that my mother never thanked or even spoke to the other moms on the block. There was a neighborhood phone list, distributed by one of the moms, but my mother never called their houses—instead she yelled from our front porch until I heard her and came running, from whosever kitchen I was in. (I kept our phone list, with other important numbers I'd added in pencil, in a drawer in the kitchen.) I was sure every family on the block stopped eating, food halfway to their mouths, waiting. The same was true of the intercom at the supermarket, and the PA system at school.

It was a long walk to Freezer's, which we shortened by cutting through the Townhouses, along the back fence of a gated community next to the Parkway, and finally through the parking lot of the Pediatric Hospital. At the edge of that parking lot there was a skinny alleyway, hidden from view, with a high gate at the end. There was a deadbolt on the gate, which had been broken and repaired so many times that we were never sure whether we'd be able to get through or have to turn back, undoing almost the entire shortcut. We always rounded the brick wall at the end of the alleyway carefully, in case whoever it was that shared our shortcut was back there, breaking through.

On the other side of the gate was the shopping center, with CVS, Blockbuster, the post office, a sushi restaurant, a bank, and Freezer's Ice Cream.

10.

Russian boys—real Russians, who didn't speak English and didn't go to our school—were sitting with one of their sisters, who was talking to Sofia on her front lawn. They were sitting in a row of lawn chairs, with paper plates in the grass next to them. We didn't want to leave without her, but we didn't want to bring the whole group of Townhouse kids with us. And if the little kids saw us leaving, our parents would make us take them along, and we'd have to go by the roads. Josef had brought his own basketball and was dribbling it around in the street.

Yeon Woo arrived from his side yard and we explained everything to him. When Sofia stood up to go inside, Peter intercepted her at her front steps.

The Huangs came outside with their skateboards. I heard the sound of the boards on the street, and turned and waved. Kenny waved back, and they started skating up the street in the other direction, practicing ollies. I stepped off the curb to follow them, and heard the sound of Josef's basketball behind me.

"Hey," he said, not looking up from his dribble.

"What's up, Josef," I said. Over his shoulder I saw Sofia talking to her dad. He pointed to their car.

"What are you doing?" he asked me. Sofia opened the car door and fiddled with something in the front seat. Then she closed the door and walked back over to her dad and handed him his wallet.

"Nothing," I said. "Skateboarding."

"When do you want to trade?" he asked me. He feinted away from me and dribbled the ball low, by his ankles.

Sofia and Peter disappeared into Paul's backyard. Paul and Yeon Woo stood in the side yard, watching me, out of view from the rest of the block.

I reached out to knock the basketball and just brushed it with my fingers. Josef slapped at it to keep it bouncing but it rolled to a stop against the curb.

"Like, tomorrow?" I said, backing away. The little kids were standing in a group under the basketball hoop. The Russians were still sitting in lawn chairs in Sofia's front yard. No one had taken Sofia's seat. Josef slapped at the basketball again. I turned and ran.

11.

The sun stayed high in the sky all afternoon. We ate our slushes on the bench in front of CVS. When we got back home, the dads were drinking Heineken.

We were playing Spud when the pervert's car pulled out of his driveway. We froze and watched, and our parents froze and watched as well. It was a blue Honda Civic. We'd already looked into all the windows, at the neat backseat and the road atlas lying flat behind the rear headrests.

He backed slowly out of his driveway. Was the car sitting low on the driver's side? He pivoted onto the street, pointing the nose of the car toward us, and paused for a long moment before putting the car in forward and turning the tires uphill, toward the intersection. On the other side of the intersection, we all watched silently. The Russian girl with the Spud ball held it tight against her chest.

He came to a full stop at the stop sign, and put on his blinker. He started to make the turn and then stopped. There were orange police barricades lined up along both sides of the intersection, blocking off the side streets from Independence. Our street hockey sticks lay in a pile next to the manhole cover. We held our breath. His car sat still, the right blinker a few feet away from the barricade, reflecting off the orange paint.

The barricades were easy to move. We'd discussed stealing one at the end of the party, so that we could close off the block whenever we liked. The only question was, who would get to keep it?

We stared at the driver's-side door. What would he be wearing? Blue jeans and an American flag t-shirt, or a short-sleeve button-down, like the dads? A prison jumpsuit? Gym shorts, like us? Naked?

And then his blinker turned off, and the car rocked slightly, and he backed up, avoiding the pile of hockey sticks. He turned his wheels down Lower Independence, drove forward over the crest of the hill, and turned back into his driveway.

12.

Kenny and Richard Huang said their piano teacher farted on the piano bench, and they could feel the vibrations. They were planning to kill him. The two of them played N64 against each other while I watched.

Downstairs, my mom and Mrs. Huang were marking up a dress in the screened-in back porch room, where Mrs. Huang had her sewing machine. Mr. Huang was watching Chinese TV in the family room. He had his own couch, with special pillows, and he lay propped up on one side because he'd been in a motorcycle accident and had scars all over his body. We'd eaten dinner in the backyard, pork dumplings and cabbage and rice with hairy pork, which was my mom's favorite.

Richard and Kenny were in a good mood tonight. We'd discussed different ways to kill the piano teacher. As the game loaded, I tried to untangle the controller cords in my mind. "Hey," I finally asked. "Do you guys know about the pervert?"

We all stared at the screen as they selected their characters.

"He's obese," Kenny said after a while.

"My mom talked to him," said Richard. His hands moved robotically on the controller. He flicked the joystick with his thumb, and pressed the buttons with his other hand using his index and middle fingers, Chinese style. Both of them had long fingernails and pointed fingers. Mrs. Huang wouldn't let them cut their nails short.

Not only that, but in the bathroom they had tooth powder instead of toothpaste. I'd had to use it one night when I slept over while my mom was away. Only later did Kenny show me where they kept the Colgate, behind the mirror. There was dried toothpaste all over the mouth of the tube. When they brushed, they kept their mouths open and let the toothpaste drip into the sink.

"He came here?" I asked, looking up at Richard's face. He puffed his lips out while he played, and his cheeks shook in rhythm with his fingers.

"He talked to my mom on the porch," Kenny said from my

other side. I sat back in my seat so that I could see both of them.

"What did he say?" I asked. Kenny got a combo on Richard and they both leaned forward in their chairs. Then Kenny said something to Richard in Chinese that sounded like "naka naka naka." Richard broke the combo and won and Kenny threw his controller across the room so hard that it came unplugged from the console. Richard stood up and turned off the N64 and the TV.

"We don't know," he said. "My mom didn't tell us."

My mother was still in the sewing room with Mrs. Huang when I went downstairs. It was dark out, and I walked to the back corner of their yard, where there was a break between the chain-link side fence and the tall wooden picket fence that separated our yards from the yards on the next street over. I slipped through the opening and into my own backyard.

13.

At the end of Lower Independence there was a gravestone store. It was at the corner where Independence met the Parkway, at the bottom of the hill, which was the end of our town. We were not allowed to cross the Parkway.

All the stones faced outward. They stood in a yard facing the street, and at the center of the yard, backed up against a steep rock wall, was the gravestone store itself.

Most of the stones were blank, but some of them had designs, mostly Celtic crosses and Jewish stars, around the space where a name or date would go. One, our favorite, was engraved with the roots of a tree reaching downward, as though toward the grave and the coffin itself.

There were only a few gravestones with writing on them. One, at the outer corner of the yard facing the intersection, said "Custom Engraving." Two smaller ones on the inside edge of the yard, facing inward, said "Rabinowitz."

Behind the store, along the base of the rock wall, was a thin alleyway. It was hidden by a chain-link fence with plastic slats in it. Inside the fence was where the owner worked on the gravestones, and those were the gravestones with names and dates, sometimes both dates and sometimes only one.

It was Josef who showed us the gravestone workshop. It was a short walk from his house, and he told us he'd explored it at night. He said he'd seen the man cutting a gravestone once, at night under a big light, using a jet of water, and that the runoff from the water jet was pinkish-grey, halfway between the color of the marble of the gravestone and the color of the asphalt where the water pooled.

From the front yard of Josef's house, I could see the edge of the gravestone yard and the first row of gravestones. I walked up the driveway and knocked lightly on the door to the basement. Josef opened it immediately and I could tell that he'd been standing on the other side of the door, waiting, when I knocked.

14.

Josef's basement had a cement floor and rock walls, like ours, though his walls were clean and painted and didn't have the flood line, a few inches off the floor, where the water rose in our basement when it stormed.

There were cardboard boxes and cases of bottled water stacked against one wall. He led me into a second room, which had a carpet and a bed and a lamp on the floor. With the light on, I could see that Josef was wearing socks and a pair of his mom's slippers that were too small for his feet. His heels hung off the back. His white t-shirt was stretched out at the neck, and he had the beginnings of a moustache growing at the corners of his lip. His sideburns went almost to the bottoms of his ears.

Josef sat cross-legged on the floor and I sat on the edge of the bed. From there I saw that he was wearing his yarmulke.

He leaned toward me and reached between my ankles and pulled out a paper Stop & Shop bag from under the bed. He un-crinkled the mouth of the bag and I leaned over, trying to see inside. He peeked in the top of the bag himself, then set it down at his hip.

"What did you bring?" he asked, and we both looked down at the pillowcase sitting on the bed next to me.

15.

I used to come to Josef's house when I was little. I went over every day after school, sometimes in the backseat of the Corvette, and on weekend mornings when my mom went to the lab. I never knew why she picked Josef's house, when there were so many normal kids on Upper Independence, and for a while at school I was associated with his family. I never saw her speak to his parents. Then I started skipping the ride home, and instead of walking to Josef's I'd go straight to Paul Ciofani's basement or to our own house, and fish the key out of the mail slot. (I'm sure Josef's dad didn't use the PA system to find me, as my mother would have.) Instead he called my mom at work, and later she and I got into an argument. I told her that Josef was retarded and that his sister Roni peed the bed and that their garage smelled like cigarettes. After that I started going straight home after school. Josef's dad still waved to me in the carpool lane, but I avoided him and the rest of the family.

Josef and Roni still shared a bedroom upstairs. In the past few years, she had become popular in her grade at school. She was in the bedroom now, on the phone with someone. We'd heard the phone ring, and felt Roni jump off the bed to pick it up.

Peter was probably on the phone with Sofia. Yeon Woo was on the computer: I'd seen the glow through the window, in the den where he always sat with the lights off. Paul would be getting homework help from his dad. My mother was sitting in the kitchen at home, listening to a book on tape and cutting the shoulder pads out of the ladies' jackets she'd bought at the Salvation Army.

16.

We traded a few small things. I gave Josef some action figures for a Nerf gun. We looked at each other's Pogs. Some of the toys we had were the same. We traded Magic cards for a while, but neither of us really knew how to play or which types of cards were valuable. All of our Magic cards had come from the same yard sale in the neighborhood just past the Townhouses. Then Josef reached under the bed again and pulled out a white towel with something long bundled in it. I quit rummaging in my pillowcase.

Josef pulled back the edge of the towel and I opened my mouth. It was rolled up, but I recognized the white-green surface. It was the Nickelodeon Flash Screen. They didn't sell them anymore, because they gave you seizures.

Josef unrolled the screen. At the center of the roll was the orange plastic lightning bolt, shaped to hang on the top of a door. It was attached to the screen by black strings. He stood up and held the screen up by the lightning bolt, and we waited as it unspun itself.

My cousins had one. Josef laid the screen back down on the floor.

"Josef," I whispered. "Do you have the Zapper?"

"Of course," he said, and reached down again into his bag. He handed to me a blue, wedge-shaped plastic remote with a flash-bulb at the fat end. I felt its weight. It had the batteries in it.

"My uncle gave it to me for Hanukkah," he said. "It's pretty boring."

"Yeah," I said. The screen had minor crease marks. There was a small knot in one of the black lines that connected it to the orange hanger.

"Yeah," I said again. I handed it back to Josef, and he held it up close to his face, as though his eyes were bad. Then he flipped a switch on the side. The Zapper hummed to life. We stared at it as it warmed up. The humming rose in pitch, and a green light lit up on the front, next to the flashbulb. Josef held it up in front of my eyes and it exploded in light.

As my vision returned, the first thing I made out was a glowing tetrahedron on the floor next to my feet. It was the screen, flaked on itself, partly covered by Josef's towel, alive with a whitish-green glow. I blinked and Josef's face came into focus. He was grinning.

"It works," I said. He put down the Zapper and flattened out the screen with his slipper. The areas that had been shielded from the flash looked dark purple against the glowing stripes.

"So," he said, taking off his slipper and pulling up his sock. "Did you get the duck?"

He meant the Beanie Baby mini duck from McDonald's. It was impossible to get in Massachusetts. It was in one out of a thousand Happy Meals. To get the complete set, which was worth a lot of money, you needed the duck, and without it the other animals were worthless.

In California, though, it was the other way around. There, the duck was one of the common ones. And I'd gone to California earlier in the summer. I went to McDonald's six times while I was there, and got three goldfish, a lizard, a lamb, and a duck. Josef knew about the trip.

I had the duck in a Ziploc freezer bag at the bottom of the pillowcase, wrapped in a dishtowel along with the other nine animals in the complete set. The room was still swimming, and I rubbed my eyes. The screen glowed faintly on the floor. I didn't say anything for a minute. Then something occurred to me and I stopped toeing the corner of the towel and looked up at Josef.

"Hey," I asked. "Did the pervert ever come to your house?"

Josef wrinkled his nose and scratched his yarmulke.

"What pervert?" he asked.

"You know," I said. "The pervert. He moved into the witch's house."

"What's the witch's house?" Josef asked. He glanced down again at the pillowcase between my feet.

17.

It was hard to know what my mom thought about the pervert. If she really was retired from parenting, then maybe she didn't care at all. I suspected that she didn't. My rules hadn't changed when he arrived, but I hadn't had many rules to begin with. I got five dollars for every A I earned in Math and Science, and ten dollars for every A+. I was not supposed to spend money on girls, because it perpetuated the stereotype that they were needy. And I was expected to come home when it got dark so that my mother didn't have to look for me. She had arthritis in her hips and had trouble standing up after she'd sat down. I wondered if she really cared where I was. I didn't get actual cash anymore for the grades; it just went on the tally that I took out of the piano bench. I bought things for girls as often as I could. Some nights, if we ate separately, or if I stayed late at the Huangs' after dinner, I discovered that my mother had gone to bed without laying eyes on me. On those nights I stayed up as late as I could, playing computer games in the den, until the house suddenly became scary.

I searched for something else that Josef might like. Near the bottom I'd packed some old video games: Sega and N64 games that I didn't play anymore, a racing game that I had two of, and a fighting game that I'd ended up with after accidentally returning one of my own games in the Blockbuster box.

The full set wasn't actually that valuable, according to my mother. I'd revealed it to her when I got back from California. She said it was a gimmick, and asked me whom I planned to sell it to. "Collectors," I said, and she said "Good luck." None of us actually knew for a fact that we could get money for it, but there was something powerful about seeing the whole group of them together. The only other place we'd seen it was at McDonald's, in the photo above the Happy Meal display case. Even the display only had, physically, three of the most common ones: the flamingo, the bull, and the lizard. We assumed the employees would have stolen the duck a long time ago. I looked at Josef's big hands, and tightened my ankle grip on the pillowcase. Through the cracked window, I could hear the whoosh of trucks driving fast down the Parkway at the bottom of Independence.

"Have you ever played Wave Race?" I asked, pulling out the stack of cartridges. He didn't have N64, but I knew that he sometimes used the one at the Jewish Center. "Or you can sell them to Blockbuster or GameStop." I held the stack out but he didn't take it.

"My mom won't let me sell games anymore," he said. He craned his neck to see into the pillowcase. I rooted around, feeling for something I'd forgotten about. The reflection of headlights passed slowly across the far wall, and a second later they glared against the glass of the window. I asked Josef if I could see the Zapper one more time.

He handed it to me and I flipped the switch. It hummed and then whirred and the green light came on. I held my foot over the corner of the screen and aimed the Zapper. I pressed the button.

We rubbed our eyes and the room resolved around us. At the corner of the screen, glowing whitish-green, was the perfect outline of my shoe and laces. I put down the Zapper and reached into my pillowcase. Josef smiled. I pulled out the Ziploc bag. I'd pressed the air out of it when I packed it, and it was crinkled around the shape of the rolled up package. I broke the seal and I thought I could hear Josef inhale as the air rushed in.

For a while we played in the basement. We turned off the light and took flashes of the complete set lined up on his arm. His hands were so big that he could hold five in each palm, and I took a flash of him like that. From up the block, we heard the sounds of different telephones ringing. Josef took the Zapper from me and turned it upside down. There was a small lightbulb at the end, which lit up when he held another small button I hadn't noticed before, and he used it to draw glowing bunny ears on the head of his silhouette. We drew other animals. We took flashes of shadow puppets, and drew faces on them.

We both saw it at the same time: red and blue lights, flickering against the far wall of the basement.

18.

We jumped off the bed and ran to the window. Standing on the washing machine, we could see, through cobwebs and a mesh of grass, the front yard and the street in front of Josef's house. A police car, with its lights on, rolled silently up Lower Independence. It drifted out of our view from the little window and I stared at the pattern of flashing lights trailing behind it on the asphalt, waiting to see where it would stop. Or was the scene of the crime somewhere else, past the intersection? Josef had climbed down off the washing machine and was staring at me.

"It's the pervert," I told him.

He had the duck cradled in both of his big hands.

"He's perverted someone in the neighborhood." I pressed my cheek to the cold glass, straining to see. When I looked back, Josef's face hadn't changed.

There were no other windows on the street side of the room. I looked around for a TV, and then remembered the shower radio I'd brought from Morgan's room. Josef walked across the basement to the bed and picked up the moose, placing it gently in his palm next to the duck. Then he turned both animals around to face me.

"Did you tell your mom you were coming over?" he asked.

I looked at the Beanie Babies and regretted trading them.

He asked again: "Did you talk to your mom before you left?" I wondered how his yarmulke stayed on his head, even when he bent down to pick up the turtle.

"My parents know you're here," he said. I pushed the switch on the Zapper and it began to hum.

We usually stayed away from Lower Independence. We couldn't play games here, because of the hill, and we didn't know the backyards or the insides of the houses. On Upper, we threw water balloons at cars that drove any faster than what we thought was safe. Down here, cars sometimes turned off from the Parkway and idled at the corner. And there was the witch's house, and the gravestone store, and squirrels froze to death here in the winter. There was a hole in the stop sign that looked to us like it was from a bullet.

"If you didn't tell your mom, she probably got worried again," Josef said, talking to me from across the room. "I don't think she knows we're friends still." The three animals fit easily on his palm.

"Do you want my dad to call her?" he asked. I walked over to the basement door and turned the knob. Outside, the air was muggy, and I itched my tongue against the roof my throat. Josef stepped through the doorway behind me. We walked through the gravel to the end of the driveway. Two yards away, the windows of the witch's house glowed blue around the edges of the blinds. Past the intersection, on Upper Independence, the red and blue lights from the cruiser flickered against the hedges in our front yard. It was parked at the end of our driveway, and I could see that our front door was open behind the screen, and that the mudroom light was on.

"It's your mom," Josef whispered.

"It's the pervert," I whispered back, hushing him. The light was on in Josef's family room, and I could see the shadows of his parents moving behind the curtains.

Just behind our hedges was a cherry tree, which I'd picked out with my mom at Home Depot. It wasn't supposed to mature for several years, but I still checked it for fruit every few weeks. Somewhere up the block another phone rang, and in the silence that followed, when it didn't ring again, I felt the whir of the Zapper in my hand. Josef and I stood at the end of his driveway, grinding our toes into the gravel and waiting.

Aphorisms for a Lonely Planet

by Lance Larsen

It is easier to photosynthesize than to say I'm sorry.

What we lack possesses us.

A side of sad gives joy its curious twang.

To go far enough you must first go too far.

Agnostic: one who takes all doubts on faith.

Modesty seduces.

First kiss: what we repent of by stealing a second, then a third . . .

When caught, water snakes pee on their captors. Politicians explain.

Prophet: one who preaches the past using future tense.

Slam a door five hundred times, one tentative turn will open it.

There I go again, ducking the snowball my brother didn't throw at me forty-two years ago, with a rock that wasn't hidden inside.

Punch line of a Yiddish joke I've forgotten: "Oedipus Schmedipus, so long as the boy loves his mother."

Attendant at the animal shelter showing me a six-toed cat: "That Hemingway character bred them," she said. "I think he was a writer or something."

My problems, I say, my addiction, my childhood baggage, my psychosomatic illness leaving me curled in the fetal position in a restaurant bathroom sobbing. As if I owned them.

Expedition Notes

by Carrie Bennett

[The expedition begins]

I learned to name objects by feel. Grass has many secrets. Certain shallow grooves meant the tree would betray me. A scaly bark meant callousness, refusal. I bent close to the ground to be near the earth. Some moss was soft as gosling feathers, though I knew better than to lay my head down. I had been warned by the locals to resist tiredness. After thunderstorms clouds could turn to falling rocks. I strapped soft bags of water on my back. I would need to learn to half-sleep standing up, always alert for the leaf that could fell me.

The expedition would take years. The locals told me I was the first woman they'd seen alone.

[Inside the canyon are many echoes]

They told me to keep running
until I saw a shining-sign
that would have a map
to the glass carnival. Each time

I almost reached the sign,
it faded further into the distance
like a metal mirage. I painted
my eyelids into bright finches.

I tried to trick the sky and
the machines above the clouds.
Across the river floated an enormous
marble head with missing eyes.

A single chair stood on the riverbank.
When I sat down my hands
turned into paper boats.
The sun set like wingless birds.

[The glass carnival]

Everyone in this new city lives in hospitals.
The buildings are sheets of glass. Sky-patterns

move slowly across the windowed-walls,
a moving lake. The hospital rooms are like

terrible elevators. Everyone eats through tubes
attached to their stomachs, a thick off-white

formula pushes through their bodies
all night. Their hands reach for me as I walk

out the door. I have searched everywhere
for food but the stores are like coffins.

Farms haven't existed for years, are mere
memory-relics. I have one cup of rice left.

A wolf started following me today. I felt
her sharp movement behind me all afternoon.

Astronomy

by Mitchell Krochmalnik Grabois

1.

I was born in the Bronx, our building destined to become a burned-out tenement populated by rats, crack heads, meth heads, severed heads. We fled to the suburbs.

In Jersey, kids coveted penny loafers and the *coolest* madras shirts. Shapiro humiliated Steven C in Plymouth Park Candy Store, because he was wearing green socks.

The aerospace industry moved west. So did we. In southern Cal you could surf and smoke pot, but the air was unbreathable.

In Berkeley, the streets were lined with cars. Their windows fed me my distorted reflection. I got fat on it.

In Humboldt County, the coastal redwoods renewed my ugly soul. I worked in a sawmill and got pneumonia four times. I found a wife and baby, but not a decent job.

In the Florida panhandle, I ate catfish and collards washed down with Jack Daniels, but race hate was tangled in the Spanish Moss. My wife took me by the hand and pulled me to the end of the road.

Key West. Our housed teemed with cockroaches, lizards and our kids' friends, Caribs, Cubans, Conchs, but even in "Paradise" bosses were unremitting assholes.

We retired to the family farm, lived on a dirt road between fields of corn and soybeans, swam in frigid Lake Michigan. I never suspected I would love being a Midwestern farmer, but corrupt commissioners plunked an outdoor turbine factory in our midst, called it a "wind farm," as if that made it agricultural. The spinning, the flutter, the subsonic vibration made us sick.

We sold the farm, beat an exit. Our kids had made a bed for us in Denver, downtown shining to the east, mountains snow-covered to the west. I rescue abused dogs and walk them in the park. Blacks and Mexicans approach and I say "Friend… friend." The walkers smile. The dog doesn't growl. He knows a treat's coming if he's a friend to all.

2.

My ninety-year-old father dreams of women, their long limbs in his bed, of drinking tequila in a little Mexican town where he and his girl buy a photo of Jesus whose eyes move from side to side. My father puts it on the dresser next to the cigarette burns, and Jesus watches him and his lady hump for hours.

My ninety-year-old father dreams of a world without nuclear power, without any power at all. He lives in the woods with his lady. They gather nuts and berries and sometimes find a fish in a free-running stream. Sometimes he takes his little green boat and rows to Japan, where the Pacific is not radiated with nuclear run-off, but is clean and hums with the songs of the fishes. One school of carp tries to make it as an *a capella* group, but they suck and they know it. They laugh at themselves, almost choke with laughter. My father laughs uncontrollably and falls out of the boat into the pleasantly warm water, and awakes to find he's peed the bed again.

3.

In Venice, scientists meet to discuss how Mars was the "in" place to kick-start life billions of years ago. Atoms came together, went red, partied hard, woke in the morning all hung over, unknown molecules, all blonde and blowsy drowsy, next to them in bed, Lolitas growing slowly into RNA, DNA, proteins.

Atom got up, brewed coffee, made Lolita a breakfast of fried eggs and toast, looked out the kitchen window at the red dust, was pleased he'd moved out here, watched Lolita open the outhouse door, sighed with happiness.

(Somewhere in the middle of all this, the astronomers find time to give my father, a noted astronomer, a lifetime award.)

The scientists leave their meeting, walk out into St. Mark's Square, which is flooded. They wade toward the Church of Santa Maria della Salute, its architecture encoded with passages from the Kabbalah; a geologist has told them *Doctor Atomic* is having its Italian premiere.

ESPERANTISTS

ESPERANTO IS THE MOST WIDELY-SPOKEN CONSTRUCTED LANGUAGE IN THE WORLD. IT WAS DEVELOPED IN THE LATE 19TH CENTURY BY L.L. ZAMENHOF, A POLISH-LITHUANIAN-RUSSIAN-JEWISH DOCTOR.

THE DIVERSITY OF LANGUAGES IS THE FIRST, OR AT LEAST THE MOST INFLUENTIAL BASIS FOR THE SEPARATION OF THE HUMAN FAMILY INTO **GROUPS OF ENEMIES.**

HE SAW A NEUTRAL, UNIVERSAL LANGUAGE AS ESSENTIAL FOR **WORLD PEACE!**

SO MY FATHER FOUND AN ESPERANTO COURSE IN "DIE NEUE VOLKSHOCHSCHULE" AND TAUGHT HIMSELF FROM IT.

ESPERANTO AMUZAJ FAKTOJ
(ESPERANTO FUN FACTS)

ZAMENHOF FIRST CALLED HIS LANGUAGE "LINGVO INTERNACIA" (INTERNATIONAL LANGUAGE), BUT THE PSEUDONYM HE PUBLISHED UNDER, "DOKTORO ESPERANTO" (DOCTOR HOPEFUL) BECAME SO POPULAR THAT HE CHANGED THE NAME!

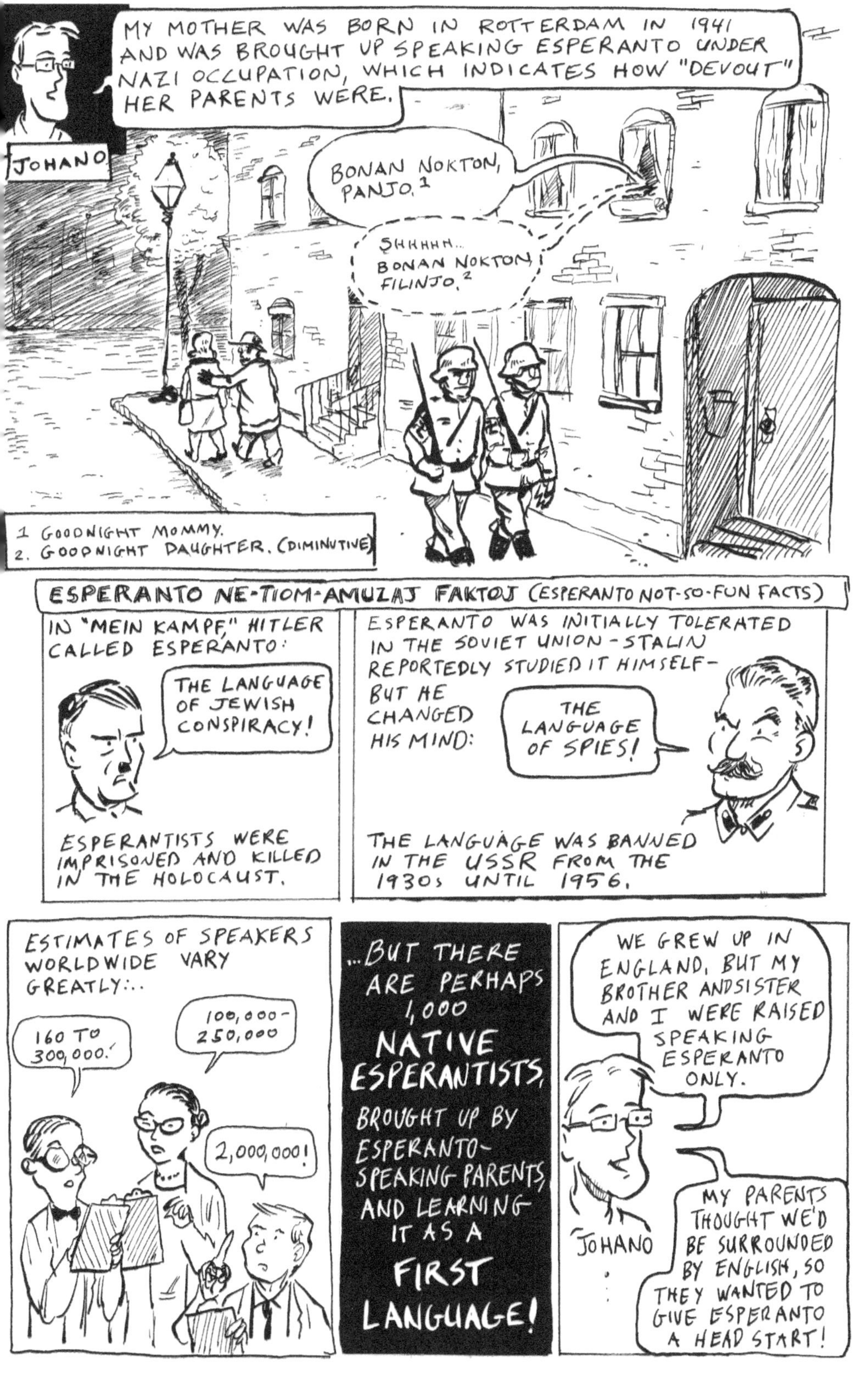

ESPERANTO NE-TIOM-AMUZAJ FAKTOJ (ESPERANTO NOT-SO-FUN FACTS)

JOHANO
I HAVE MEMORIES OF HAVING TO TRANSLATE BETWEEN MY LITTLE SISTER AND OUR ENGLISH GRANDPARENTS.
ĈU VI ŜATAS MIAN HUNDIDON?
SHE SAYS, DO YOU LIKE HER PUPPY DOG?
IT STRUCK ME AS SURREAL EVEN THEN!
THE FIRST ESPERANTO UNIVERSALA KONGRESO (UNIVERSAL CONGRESS) WAS HELD IN FRANCE IN 1905. THEY HAVE BEEN HELD EVERY YEAR SINCE (EXCEPT DURING THE WORLD WARS.)
THE ESPERANTO FLAG (GREEN AND WHITE)
BUDAPEST 1966
MONTEVIDEO 1954
GOTHENBURG 1918
BERN 1913
KONGRESO ESPERANTO MONDO BUDAPESTO 1966
ERIC KUAN
1ª UNIVERSALA ESPERANTO EKSPOZICIO
MONTEVIDEO
NOVEMBRO-DEC. 1954
GOTENBURGO 6-10 AUG. 1918
UNUA SKANDINAVA KONGRESO DE ESPERANTO
IX. UNIVERSALA KONGRESO DE ESPERANTO BERN, 24-31 Aŭgusto 1913
IN ADDITION, THERE ARE MANY REGIONAL CONFERENCES, YOUTH EVENTS, AND EVEN CHILDREN'S CONGRESSES.
ESPERANTO
AS CHILDREN, OUR HOLIDAYS WERE ALWAYS TO ESPERANTO EVENTS. MY MUM HELPED RUN ONE OF THE CHILDREN'S CONGRESSES — BETWEEN 40 AND 100 KIDS, FROM 25-35 DIFFERENT COUNTRIES, ALL AT A SORT OF SUMMER CAMP.

¹·SUTURE (ESPERANTO) ²·SUTURE (GERMAN)

FOR MY FATHER, IT WAS A WAY OUT OF A COUNTRY THAT THERE WAS NO WAY OUT OF. WE LIVED IN TOMSK, IN THE USSR. IT WAS A CLOSED CITY; YOU COULDN'T LEAVE UNLESS SOMEONE OFFICIALLY INVITED YOU. SO THANKS TO ESPERANTO...

...I GOT TO VISIT YUGOSLAVIA AND BULGARIA WHEN I WAS SEVEN.

WE COULDN'T AFFORD HOTELS, SO HAVING ESPERANTO FRIENDS EVERYWHERE WAS THE ONLY WAY.

I WAS THIS CHILD WONDER WHEREVER I'D GO, THIS LITTLE GIRL WHO COULD SPEAK FASTER THAN ANYONE, WHO'D CORRECT PEOPLE ON THEIR GRAMMAR. I GOT TO SEE SO MANY PLACES, MEET SO MANY PEOPLE... I THINK I HAD A TOTALLY DIFFERENT PERCEPTION OF THE WORLD THAN MOST KIDS AT THAT AGE.

ESPERANTO AMUZAJ FAKTOJ

THERE ARE OVER 250,000 ESPERANTO BOOKS IN PRINT, BOTH TRANSLATIONS AND ORIGINAL WORKS. COMICS AVAILABLE IN ESPERANTO INCLUDE TINTIN, TEZUKA'S PHOENIX; BAREFOOT GEN, AND EVEN ONE OF JACK CHICK'S RELIGIOUS TRACTS!

*HEY KIDS, COMICS!

LET'S HEAR FROM A NON-NATIVE!!
I WAS A NERDY KID, GROWING UP IN NORTH CAROLINA, READING THE WORLD BOOK ENCYCLOPEDIA...
WOW! AN INVENTED LANGUAGE?!
JULIE AGE 39
AS A KID, WORLD PEACE AND UNDERSTANDING SOUNDED PRETTY COOL, AND AS A MATH GEEK, PLAYING WITH LANGUAGE AS A PUZZLE DID TOO!

I SENT AWAY FOR A CORRESPONDENCE COURSE -- A TUTOR CORRECTS YOUR WORK AND SENDS IT BACK.
UNITED STATES POSTAL SERVICE

I DIDN'T FINISH THE COURSE (I HAD A LOT MORE ENTHUSIASM THAN DILIGENCE AT THAT AGE), SO I STILL DIDN'T REALLY SPEAK THE LANGUAGE WHEN I GOT TO COLLEGE, AND ATTENDED THE FIRST MEETING OF THE MIT ESPERANTO SOCIETY...
FRESHMAN, HUH?
WE'RE ALL GRADUATING THIS YEAR...
MIT

...SO YOU'RE THE NEW PRESIDENT!!
MIT

SO THE NEXT YEAR I WAS PRESIDENT OF THE CLUB... AND THE ONLY MEMBER!
STUDENT ACTIVITIES
ESPERANTO SOCIETY

WHEN WE GOT TOO OLD FOR THE CHILDREN'S CONGRESSES, WE'D GO TO THE YOUTH EVENTS...
... AND PARTY.
JOHANO
OFTEN THE ORGANIZERS WOULD UNDER-ESTIMATE THE NUMBERS, AND A YOUTH HOSTEL WITH 200 BEDS WOULD HAVE 500 KIDS IN IT.
I BUILT MUCH OF MY LIFE AROUND THESE EVENTS, MEETING THE SAME PEOPLE, WITH A FEW ADDITIONS EACH TIME, ENDING UP WITH VARIOUS GIRLFRIENDS...
POR DANCADI LA BAMBON, POR DANCADI LA BAMBON, NECESAS JE KULERETO DA ĈARMO KULERETO DA ĈARMO, KUN PETOLEMO...*
* "LA BAMBA" IN ESPERANTO

JULIE
I REMEMBER MY FIRST YOUTH CONFERENCE. A BUNCH OF US WERE AT A TABLE, TALKING, HAVING FUN... AND I SUDDENLY REALIZED...
NONE OF US CAME FROM THE SAME LANGUAGE! I HAD TOTALLY FORGOTTEN!
IF I WASN'T ENTHUSIASTIC ABOUT SCHOOL OR THE PEOPLE THERE, I'D THINK OF MY FRIENDS ABROAD, AND EXCHANGE LETTERS.
STELA
STEFFI GRAF
...mi vidos vin baldaŭ, mi esperas. *
WHEN I READ THEM, I WOULDN'T CARE SO MUCH HOW CRAPPY IT IS TO BE A TEENAGER!
*...see you soon, I hope.
JULIE
"INTIMATE RELATIONSHIPS" IN ESPERANTO? ...YES... THERE'S BEEN SOME... EXPLORATION.
THAT'S WHEN YOU REALIZE WHAT A REAL LANGUAGE IT IS...
ĈU TIO ESTAS BONA?
IOM PLI MALRAPIDE...
...KIEL ĈI TIO?
HHHHOOO... JJJESSSS... (SUSPIRO)

ESPERANTO AMUZAJ FAKTOJ!

IN 1967, THE REPUBLIC OF ROSE ISLAND, A SELF-DECLARED "SOVEREIGN STATE" ON A 4000 SQ-FT PLATFORM IN THE ADRIATIC SEA, BECAME THE FIRST COUNTRY TO MAKE ESPERANTO ITS OFFICIAL TONGUE.
JES!
ESPERANTUJO?*
UNFORTUNATELY, THE ITALIAN GOVERNMENT DEMOLISHED THE "NATION" IN 1968.
*"ESPERANTO LAND?" "YES!"

ABOUT FIVE YEARS AGO, I BURNED OUT AND QUIT THE ESPERANTO SCENE.
I FINALLY STARTED LIVING IN THE REAL WORLD, WITH A STABLE JOB, A MORTGAGE, A NICE CAR, AND A WONDERFUL WIFE.
JOHANO

I KNOW MANY PEOPLE WHO HAVE THE BEST REASONS FOR LEARNING ESPERANTO, AND BEING INVOLVED. AND THEN YOU HAVE THE SAD, LONELY LOSERS, DESPERATE TO FIND SOMETHING TO ATTACH IDENTITY TO, AND THE MORE "ESPERANTO" THEY ARE, THE MORE ACCEPTED THEY FEEL.

AND IT FRUSTRATES THE HELL OUT OF ME THAT IT'S ALL BASED ON AN IDEAL WHICH CAN'T REALLY COME TO PASS.

AH, THE "INTERNAL IDEA!" THERE ARE STILL SPECIMENS OF THAT TYPE - THE BELIEF THAT ONCE WE ALL HAVE A COMMON LANGUAGE, WORLD PEACE IS INEVITABLE! WELL, THE AMERICAN CIVIL WAR, THE TWO GERMANIES, THE TWO KOREAS TELL US A DIFFERENT STORY! AS, TO BE HONEST, DO THE QUARRELS WITHIN ESPERANTO SOCIETIES THEMSELVES!
PETER

BUT ESPERANTO IS STILL THE BEST INSTRUMENT OF INTERNATIONAL COMMUNICATION— FOR PEOPLE WHO ARE ALREADY OPEN-MINDED BEFORE THEY COME TO IT!

I GOT OUT JUST IN TIME TO NOT END UP ONE OF THOSE GUYS STILL GOING TO YOUTH EVENTS IN THEIR FIFTIES, OGLING THE GIRLS, WEARING MULTIPLE FIVE-POINTED GREEN STAR BADGES AND WONDERING WHAT THE BLOODY HELL HAPPENED TO THEIR LIVES!

I TOOK MY WIFE TO AN ESPERANTO EVENT. I TAUGHT HER ONE PHRASE:
FORFIKIĜU, STRANGULO!*
SHE USED IT MANY TIMES UNDER HER BREATH. PROBABLY AT ME A FEW TIMES! * "FUCK OFF, WEIRDO"

WE CAN PROVE THAT ESPERANTO IS MUCH EASIER TO LEARN THAN ANY NATIONAL LANGUAGE. AT A UNIVERSITY LEVEL, IT'S 40 TIMES EASIER TO LEARN THAN ENGLISH, WHICH IS USED AS AN INSTRUMENT OF MODERN IMPERIALISM!

AND THEN, WE ALL COMPLAIN ABOUT TAXES! WELL, THE EU PARLIAMENT HAS NOW 23 OFFICIAL LANGUAGES. A SWISS ECONOMIST* HAS SHOWN THAT THIS COSTS 25 BILLION EURO A YEAR!
*FRANCOIS GRIN, UNIVERSITY OF LUGANO, IN A 2005 STUDY.

YOU MIGHT HAVE THE IMPRESSION I'M THE ENEMY OF ENGLISH. I'M NOT. I JUST DON'T SEE WHY WE CHOOSE THE POOREST OF ALL SOLUTIONS TO THE LANGUAGE PROBLEM.

BUT DON'T TAKE MY WORD FOR IT: UMBERTO ECO SAID,* "ESPERANTO COULD WORK AS A WORLD LANGUAGE. FROM ALL OBJECTIONS, ONLY ONE REMAINS: 'THE EGOISM OF GOVERNMENTS'."
*ECO, "THE SEARCH FOR THE PERFECT LANGUAGE"

MOST PEOPLE DON'T EXPECT THAT THE WHOLE WORLD WILL SPEAK IT. IF THEY DO, GREAT.
OR MAYBE NOT. MAYBE IF MORE PEOPLE SPOKE IT IT WOULDN'T BE AS COOL!
JULIE

LANA
PERSONALLY, I DON'T WANT EVERYONE TO SPEAK ESPERANTO, EVER. I DON'T THINK IT SHOULD BE MANDATORY IN SCHOOLS. I LIKE IT THAT WHEN I MEET PEOPLE, I KNOW THEY'VE MADE THE EFFORT TO FIND THE BOOKS, TO LEARN IT.
BONAN NOKTON, PANJO
THAT TAKES A LOT OF COURAGE, A LOT OF INITIATIVE ...
...THAT'S THE KIND OF PEOPLE I WANT TO MEET!
THANKS TO ALL THE ESPERANTISTS WHO TOOK PART IN THIS STORY!!
LOOKS LIKE THERE'S TIME FOR ONE MORE
ESPERANTO AMUZAJ FAKTOJ:
THE 1965 HORROR FILM, INCUBUS, WAS FILMED ENTIRELY IN ESPERANTO. IT STARRED WILLIAM SHATNER!
TRANSVENIGU MIN, SKOTĈJO!
*"BEAM ME UP, SCOTTY."

I Blog Therefore I Am

by Judy Kugel

Eighteen years ago I started a journal to document what I thought would be my last year of relative youth. I was fifty-nine. My sixties loomed, a decade I dreaded that turned out to be quite wonderful. Our children were educated, my career was chugging along, my health was excellent. My husband and I traveled extensively, mostly by bicycle. I studied Spanish for the first time, published several travel articles in magazines and newspapers, discovered a half-sister I never knew about, and became a grandmother.

A month before my seventieth birthday, with the blogosphere in full bloom, I decided to publicly document my journey through my eighth decade. Having been lucky enough to make it to seventy, the odds were that I would have many good years left. But the promise of my seventies was clouded by the realization that my future was getting shorter.

In my opening post, in January of 2008, I invited the reader to "join me on a journey into my seventies," predicting "some sad things—a given as we age," but also an attempt to "embrace change and appreciate each day." I added:

I'll probably write about my parents and being a parent. I'll write about the role exercise plays in my life and should play in yours. I'll share my thoughts about aging in the workplace. I'll report on my efforts to catalogue my wrinkles. And more. Please stay tuned.

Since I wrote those words, I've blogged at 70-something.com twice a week, about 850 posts. Sometimes, only 150 words. But something. And though I don't have a Beyoncé-sized following, my average daily views have increased exponentially. Considering that I started with about ten followers, exponentially wasn't hard.

Deciding What to Write

How do I decide what to write? I listen to myself. What has captured my attention? What has kept me up at night? What scares me? What makes me laugh? What do I love? How do I react to new wrinkles? What have I read, listened to, watched that I think people should hear about?

Writing a blog is about noticing the first crocus, or our three-year-old neighbor Christian yelling "good-bye!" in red-and-white-striped pajamas on the sidewalk as his dad goes off to work. It's about documenting the ups and downs in relationships, and how technology has changed my life. Knowing that I have to have something to say makes me pay closer attention.

When do my ideas come to me? Often on long walks, especially if I am walking with my husband, whom regular readers have come to know pretty well. He gets praised (mostly), kidded (often) and is loved (always) in my blog. Once a year he does a guest appearance–I'm not sure how that started. Sometimes an idea comes to me while I am exercising on my foam roller. Or sometimes I see something or experience something that cries out to be blogged about. One recent example described a trip to the airport and my reactions to two very different bus passengers – a sad, disheveled (probably) homeless man and an adorable toddler who chatted happily with me and bid me good-bye when he got off. My blog closed with this rueful reaction:

> One passenger who seems to have lost his way in life. Another, with so much in front of him. Hope and despair on a short bus ride....

Sometimes a snippet of conversation that I hear, remember, and write down turns into a blog post; sometimes it doesn't. For example, I was astonished to learn that our eleven-year-old grandson had given up drinking soda. Not because his parents insisted. Or because he wanted to be healthy or save his teeth. He gave it up because his soccer coach thought he should. I felt this was a worthy subject. But somehow, it never made the cut.

There are some subjects that don't get much of my "air" time. For example, only one title has the word "sex" in it. That's because as a member of The Silent Generation, it's not something I blab (or blog) about. I also haven't written much about religion or politics. At least not yet.

Some days, my post practically writes itself. Here's one that says it all in four lines:

Insomnia

> In the middle of the night, the slightest headache is an incipient brain tumor, a child not-heard-from has been abducted, a work concern is a full-blown crisis, and I'll never have an idea for another blog entry.
> In the morning...all is well.

What you Learn

Through my blog I have watched myself age. In the first years, I wrote a lot about my job, but lately I write more about living as fully as possible, about not doing what I don't want to do, knowing that the arc of my life is getting shorter, and I will be able to do less, not more as I grow older. My retirement was a huge turning point, and my posts reflected how I struggled to adjust to the loss of community. I was able to fill the void in a positive way, but it took a while. Writing about it more than twenty times helped me process all of that. I kept finding new angles. For example, I drew a connection between summer camp, where on the last night they served roast beef so campers went home to report wonderful meals to their parents, and my career, where after retirement I tend to savor memories of only the good parts.

How Personal Should You Get?

I have learned that writing something makes it real. I think that is why it was so hard for me to acknowledge in print that my husband Peter has Parkinson's Disease. Eight years ago that diagnosis was also a turning point. And although there are some things we can't do anymore, we focus on what we can do. Here's an excerpt from that post:

P.D.

It took a retired doctor whom Peter barely knew to suggest Parkinson's Disease....

The good news was that the wondering about what was going on was over. The bad news was that we were faced with a serious disease that has a lot of uncertainty related to it. We had no idea about how the disease would progress. Would Peter's quality of life change significantly? Would we need to move out of our house? Would we have to curtail our active lifestyle? There is no answer that works for everyone, but everyone wants an answer....

Peter used to remind me that we always forget to say "I'm fortunate because my big toe is not hurting today."

Well, my big toe doesn't hurt today.

I have learned how lucky I am. I have learned that I shouldn't take that luck for granted.

Then There's the Question of Who You're Sharing With

I don't know my readers. I was at first sure they were all in their 60s or 70s, but I heard from a young newlywed who said she is taking lessons about marriage from my experience. I have heard from 40-year-olds. Much to my surprise, I've heard from a number of male readers.

I keep a "Blog" email file. In it are comments from readers I don't know who have told me that they relate to or are moved by what I write. Although I started the blog to help myself process growing older, comments arrive such as "Thank you for your lovely posts. I connect, on some level, with almost all of them," or "Sometimes when I read your blog, I wonder if you know your impact! Thanks for writing." Or: "All teary (again!) from this post ☺ Your attitude towards life and living is marvelous – here's to many more blogging years." Or: "Lovely beyond words… Thanks for sharing your husband, your accomplishments, your hopes and fears and, especially, your joys. The 70s are full of change and challenge and it's nice to have your companionship as I begin them."

Occasionally someone is disappointed, like the woman who commented that I didn't take into account those who are alone when I wrote about the holidays. I apologized in my next post.

I love that I can connect with people. Knowing that I might be helpful to some as they navigate aging keeps me going. Nobody gave me a "how-to" book for my 70s. It's a bit like my big belly at the end of my first pregnancy. I knew that there would be a baby eventually. But I had no idea about the experience between the belly and the baby. There wasn't yet any book like *What to Expect When you're Expecting* to prepare me for labor or the raging hormones that followed. Everybody experiences childbirth a little differently. So too, aging. But I hope that my experience might give those behind me a helpful preview.

Themes Emerge from Your Life

My marriage is definitely my number one subject, with at least three dozen posts. If you add parents and children and family, it adds up to about a hundred. Although I've had a great career, family has always come first. Here are a few excerpts:

Saturday Morning Conversation

Me: "My egg has a huge crack in it."

Peter: "Oh, I didn't see it."

Me: " I know you didn't see it because you would have taken that egg. You always give me the better thing."

A Legacy for Grandchildren

We have two grandsons, ages 4 and 1½…Sadly, they don't live nearby, so we only get to see them every few months. But I want them to know us as I never got to know my own grandparents…So each time we see them, I write them a "letter" about how they have grown and changed, how proud we are of them and how much joy they bring us.

I also tell them about us. For example, after Peter's retirement party a couple of years ago, I "wrote" to them. I told them how I had learned things about their grandfather that night that I never knew… how they named a room after him at Boston College. Even the grandkids' father and uncle were saying, "Wow, we never knew that about Dad!"

My body stars in a couple dozen.

Wrinkled Like A Skeleton

Until recently, people I met took me for five to ten years younger than I am. But just last week, I noticed that the "bags" under my eyes that I thought were due to a night of insomnia hadn't gone away after a good night's sleep.

My 4½ year old grandson informed me on a recent visit that my neck "looked wrinkled like a skeleton." ...On an earlier trip, his older brother had told me that a new face cream made my face look "less wrinkly."

On the bright side, my smile is still genuine.

I didn't write about feeling older until 2011 because that's when I first saw myself as "older." I didn't start writing end-of-life thoughts until a year ago, partly because Atul Gawande eloquently raised the issue in *Being Mortal* and partly because our children need to know our wishes for care if/when we can't make decisions ourselves.

The Blogging Bonus

What I didn't know when I started blogging was that writing could be good for my health. According to *Advances in Psychiatric Treatment*, the benefits of expressive writing about trauma or emotional events result in long-term improvement in both physical and psychiatric health. Of course, you don't need to have experienced trauma to benefit from writing. An article in *Scientific American* called "Blogging—It's Good for You" claims "expressive writing produces many physiological benefits," including improved memory and sleep, boosting immune cell activity and more. Although turning seventy is not necessarily traumatic, changes like retirement, loss of loved ones, or health challenges can be. Even keeping a "gratitude journal" in which we regularly record things we are thankful for can make us happier and healthier.

Is There a Downside?

Yes. My friends who follow me "know" what I am up to. But since they don't write a blog, I can't keep up with them so easily. There's also the obligation part. I am compulsive, but sometimes it's just hard to write. I can look at the numbers of hits I get daily. That's fun, except on a day when I have fewer reads, I wonder if I am not doing so well or am getting stale. But then my number of reads always bounces back up. At least so far. Even though I don't want to care, I do.

Give it a try

Getting started is easy. There are many platforms/hosts for your blog, all discoverable through your favorite search engine. Some are free. Others charge based on the amount of bells and whistles you want. The crucial thing is to write regularly. Twice a week works for me and, although I started writing just for me and without a marketing plan, people are reading and responding. One way to build your fan club is to read and comment on the blogs of others so that they read yours.

If you join the blogosphere, you will not be alone. According to Statista, Tumblr hosts more than 246.6 million blog accounts and millions of blog posts are written daily.

Finally...

I write about life in my 70s because I love to write. An unexpected bonus is that looking at the ways my topics and perspective have changed over the past seven years helps me process the inevitable changes that come with aging.

We all face an uncharted future. We can't control what happens to us. But we can control how we react to it. And through good times and bad, the process of writing helps makes it better. As famed author Flannery O'Connor once said, "I write because I don't know what I think until I read what I say."

She's right.

Boys of Summer

by Molly Howes

In my family, being baseball fans was like being Catholic. It was simply who we were.

For as long as I can remember, we rooted for the St. Louis Cardinals. Well into adulthood, I had no idea why. Neither we nor anyone else in our family had ever lived in St. Louis. But I never questioned our loyalty, just as I would not have questioned our height (tall) or eye color (brown). Those characteristics defined us. Even the special connection I've always felt to the actual scarlet birds followed from feeling connected to the team, rather than the other way around.

I grew up with the names of the players a natural part of my language; "Stan the Man" stood for any great, solid guy; "Doing a Bob Gibson" meant whiffing someone in any sport – ping pong or Frisbee included. The force in the blunt names Lou Brock and Curt Flood, the flow in Tim McCarver and Orlando Cepeda (even Tito Francona, a name I came to love later in Boston) still give me pleasure today. I hear my brothers' exultant voices, too, in response to long-ago radio exploits. They re-enacted double plays they'd only heard from the play-by-play guy.

They knew everybody's batting averages, on-base percentages and RBIs, and I knew players' positions and which way they batted and pitched. I collected stories and rumors about my favorites, the way, later, I'd follow adored rock and roll musicians.

Just as I didn't know how the Cardinals became, as it were, nested in our family, I wasn't sure why baseball itself figured so prominently. Maybe it was having three boys in the family, all of whom played quite a bit of baseball themselves – with considerable success and a lot of style. But our devotion long predated their stints in Little League. Maybe it began when our parents lived in Boston in the late '40s, near two major league ball fields. My father had grown up in New England and had always loosely followed the Red Sox. The 1948 season, the almost-subway series, overlapped with their courtship. That year, the Red Sox almost made it to the World Series (losing in the first American League pennant playoff to Cleveland) against the Boston Braves. My parents' first apartment was in the building below the now-iconic Citgo sign in Kenmore Square, near Fenway Park. But, more likely, baseball mattered because it captured my mother's romantic sense of summer boys playing a graceful, outdoor game.

I developed a similar sense, though I also remember baseball uniform laundry, which is a lot less romantic. I scrubbed hard with my two fists inside the knees and backsides of my brothers' Little League uniforms to get that orangey baseline dirt out. I remember last minute scrambles for socks and gloves, pulled muscles, sprained wrists, and awful losses that should have turned out differently. I remember sitting for endless hours on hard stands, while next to nothing happened. But I'm getting ahead of myself here. I was talking about my family's fandom, not my brothers' actual participation in the sport.

Recently, I called my youngest brother Bob, to ask about the Cardinals. Unlike me, he knew why we rooted for them growing up. During our early family years, we had lived in Tulsa, Oklahoma. Because Tulsa was the location of the St. Louis organization's AAA team, the Cardinals were the closest thing we had to a big league home team.

When we lived in Tulsa, my parents listened to Cardinals games on the radio, so we did, too. After my father died, though, it was our highly educated, musician mother who developed the greater devotion. She listened to games in the kitchen almost every summer day. The sport began to infuse our worldview with a distinct flavor, providing ready metaphors like being "on deck" and "swinging for the fences." Looking back now, I imagine that baseball was a sort of stand-in for an adult male presence in the family. If so, she made a pretty good choice: the players appeared to be admirable and strong men, clean-cut and brave. We held our myths close to our hearts, safe from contradictory information, practically sacred.

Following my father's death, we began to move. Often. The main criterion for a new neighborhood seemed to be its Catholic Church. When we left Oklahoma for Long Island in 1960, we carried not only our Catholicism, but our St. Louis loyalty with us.

Not that New York presented any competition. The Dodgers and the Giants had already departed the city. The Yankees offered individual players to admire—Roger Maris hit 61 homers in 1961, our first full season there—but seemed privileged, fat with a success they'd achieved without our support. Like a religious tenet we all endorsed unquestioningly, in our family we didn't trust the Bronx Bombers.

Nor did 1962's embarrassingly bad expansion team, the Mets, seem likely to tempt us away. Their first year record, 40 – 120, was the worst since Major League Baseball settled on the 162 game schedule. (Two games were cancelled.) Nobody we knew longed to go to games at the Polo Grounds. None of us kids had any interest in the Mets except as the butt of jokes. It wasn't just their losing; we were as certain of the Mets' uselessness as we were of the Cardinals' essential heroism. Such baseball sensibilities had seemed to spring spontaneously (and, we thought, permanently) from deep within us.

Although we kids kept faith in the Cardinals through our frequent, abrupt moves and our mother's escalating mood swings, a mysterious shift in our mother's allegiance threatened to throw us. She began to root for the Mets. Before she left for work in the mornings – whether in spectator pumps and carrying a steno pad, or wearing a waitress uniform and white tie-up shoes – she began to leave open the sports page on the kitchen table. Converging at home after school, we'd find inked circles around paragraphs and underlinings in the stats boxes if any Mets player did anything good – rare as that was. But, in the midst of our family's worsening season, we kids, as a bloc, refused to have anything to do with the Mets. We regarded her change in team loyalty as practically blasphemous. Moreover, her newfound affection seemed out of character: Our mother definitely loved a winner. Only later would we realize she especially liked a come-from-behind winner, someone who proves other people's expectations wrong.

After many moves on Long Island, each house less stable than the last, my mother threw in the towel on keeping our struggling household going. I was nine when she headed to the proverbial showers and sent us away to an orphanage in upstate New York.

In the Children's Home, I was separated not only from my mother but from my brothers. I saw my younger brothers at school occasionally. Bobby, the youngest, endeared himself to me (and all the other girls in my grade) by hugging me in the hallways. Over the time we lived in the orphanage, Byron, seventeen months younger than I was, grew almost as tall as I and much bolder, which I found annoying.

The main occasions when I saw my older brother Bill came on Saturdays, when all the Home children were required to participate in Recreation Time. My favorite days were warm ones when the boys played ball out in the back fields. Girls rarely played any sports. Older girls watched boys from the sidelines and tried to get the boys to notice them. At first I was too young for the general boy-watching, but I kept a close eye on Bill as he played, feeling connected then, less lonely. Whether it was kickball or softball or baseball, the boys took their positions in the field and the game unfolded in a recognizable pattern. Seeing my brother move naturally, unencumbered by the heaviness he carried throughout most of our time in the orphanage, calmed me down. The game itself, with its predictable structure, settled me.

My mother wrote us occasional brief notes, addressed to all her children, in age order. After the World Series of 1963, she sent us a note announcing the "highfalutin' Yankees' comeuppance." She wrote that the Dodgers, "late of Brooklyn, with one Sandy Koufax on the mound" had bested them.

The sports pages provided a way to feel connected to her. The local paper carried mostly stories about the Yankees, but we also read shorter reports of Mets games – sometimes involving their National League opponents, the Cardinals. Our commitment to St. Louis remained clear; we felt no loyalty conflict.

But then, during the first full season we lived at the Home, a surprise arrived. Instead of a short note, we received a flat, brown-papered parcel. Inside were separate white envelopes, one labeled for each of us. In the accompanying note, our mother wrote that she had won a hundred-to-one bet on the Mets in a bar near her latest Manhattan apartment. She sent each of us a $5 bill – which to us was a considerable sum – generously sharing her winnings. After her bet, we grudgingly allowed the Mets to become a second-tier team of ours, the hard luck, underdog team, unlikely to win.

Our stay in the Children's Home stretched across a second winter and into another baseball season. On an early summer day, a picture postcard arrived. Viewed from the sidewalk, the Empire State Building zoomed from shadow into bright sun. On the back, our mother had written that she was leaving New York and heading south.

Over the next weeks, then months, additional postcards came from the New Jersey shore; Dover, Delaware; Annapolis. Her purpose was indecipherable, but we hoped she was looking for a home for us. She proceeded down the Eastern seaboard, skipping Baltimore and Washington because she never liked their baseball teams. It had become a point of some personal resentment for her that the Twins (relocated from DC) were flourishing in Minnesota. None of us can remember what she had against the Orioles. We charted her location, as we waited through most of the next baseball season, through the summer of my first crushes on boys and my first real bra. The mapped line of her travel was crooked and confusing. We couldn't determine her trajectory.

Finally, when it seemed that she was running out of states, she found us a new house. The picture she sent, a crisp black and white snapshot of a stucco cottage surrounded by strange, large-leafed plants, came from Florida. Her new town, St. Petersburg, held the distinction of hosting spring training for two major league baseball teams: the St. Louis Cardinals and the New York Mets. It seemed fated. We joined her there, in a climate that allowed baseball to be played year-round. We lived two quick blocks from the field where the Mets trained.

My brothers all played baseball for years; I became a scorekeeper for the town recreation department. Diagramming plays appealed to my sense of orderliness and my affection for capturing a story in symbols. As a scorekeeper, I could watch as much baseball as I wanted. Between plays, my primary focus on my brothers made way for growing interest in other baseball-playing boys. Nonetheless, I continued to follow my brothers as they won Little League titles.

Even our reluctantly-chosen team went on to become winners. Known as the "Miracle Mets," they won the 1969 World Series.

During our twenties, Bill traveled around the country playing semi-professional softball. One summer weekend, I showed up in Parma, Ohio, for the men's National Slow Pitch Softball Tournament. I surprised Bill at a bright green baseball field. As I approached, he leaned on a waist-high wire fence wearing his uniform of baggy trousers and three-quarter-length sleeves. He stood up in the late afternoon summer light, the kind that lingers so you don't believe the day will ever end, and hugged me tighter than he ever has, both of us laughing. I watched him play, drank a lot of beer, and yelled myself hoarse. His team, Nelson Painting, became national champs. Bill hit eleven home runs in that tournament.

Since then we've all changed our patterns. We lost Byron to an illness related to the one that killed our father young. Our mother died, too, still residing in St. Petersburg. Now, well into our middle years, Bill, Bob, and I are close. Despite living considerable distances from each other, we get together when we can. I often write about the lifestyle predilections the three of us share. We are all drawn to any body of water, for example, and usually feel compelled to submerge ourselves in it. We are avid composters. We embrace Buddhist practices. And we often watch baseball.

Bob and I root for both our own respective home teams (Boston for me, Tampa Bay for him) and each other's. It's good to have a second choice in the same league, because no team can win all their games and no team can play against the Yankees all the time. We used to talk on the phone while watching our teams play each other. Now we text, which is less annoying to our families. We still keep an occasional eye on the Cardinals. First loves and myths fade slowly.

I, who never played baseball—who, being a girl, never considered playing—still tear up when I catch a first glimpse of the emerald grass at Fenway Park. Recently, Bill visited and we attended a Red Sox game, the first time he'd been to the park since our grandfather took him as a little boy and he saw Ted Williams hit a home run. We both sniffled our way through an inning or so, before posting Facebook pictures of the two of us with Fenway signs in the background.

Baseball didn't give our lives all the structure or truth we needed as children. But the game provided a particular sensibility and a source of connection with our mother and among us. Baseball taught us about patience and rules and grace in the face of disappointment. The game remains our shared history, a pattern of wins and losses – like the ones my family encountered, like the rhythm of spring coming, reliably rich with possibility, and summer inevitably fading. Like the next season arriving again.

Return to Fort Scott: An American Hometown in Black and White

by Paul A. Tamburello, Jr.

Gordon Parks may not have had a plan when the Life magazine photographer was assigned in 1950 to visit his hometown in Fort Scott, Kansas. The first stirrings of desegregation were roiling in the South, a low indistinct rumbling quietly unsettling a way of life largely undisturbed since the Civil War. Parks felt it underfoot. Was there evidence of hope for his classmates that racial oppression could or would be overcome?

The magazine's first black photojournalist had been hired two years before. His colleagues? Names that adorn coffee table glossies… Margaret Bourke-White, Andreas Feininger, Alfred Eisenstaedt, Cecil Beaton, Robert Capa, W. Eugene Smith, to name a few. Like them, Parks had an eye for content and composition but it was his life experience that separated him most distinctly from his colleagues.

Now the Boston Museum of Fine Arts has assembled the results of his photographic journey home. *Back To Fort Scott*, a compact, affecting exhibition of meticulously printed black and white photographs, is like a grainy, retro speed bump between the museum's adjacent galleries, which feature big, bold modern art, colorful and expansive. The forty-two photographs hung on the walls of the modest Robert and Jane Burke Gallery on the third level, the images mostly 8 x 10 inches in size, require close observation.

Parks' assignment was to take the political and cultural temperature of the effect of school segregation in the South. Parks reconnected with ten of the twelve of his ninth grade classmates with whom he graduated from all-black Plaza Elementary School in 1927 and hadn't seen since.

The very first photo in the exhibit shows that Parks was interested in making strong pictorial statements. It features a middle-aged white man in farmer overalls. He stands at a train crossing in the middle of town, a speculative look on his creased face as he surveys the photographer. The "STOP" sign held in his hand is a perfect metaphor for Fort Scott, Kansas and the South in the 1950s. The hard lines of segregation are as deeply embedded in the mentality of this town as the steel railroad tracks running through the middle of town.

The photos on the four walls of the small gallery make what Parks has to say about his subjects crystal clear, even if you choose not to read a word of the background notes that accompany each print.

This is not to say that he was obvious. Parks was slyly political. He knew the power and stature of Life magazine and that white readers had little person-to-person interaction with their black counterparts. He intended to present a nuanced portrait of "negro" life that had never been seen before in a popular national publication.

His photos of couples and families were taken with backgrounds of front doors, front porches or living rooms, all signs of stability. If you substituted white for black skin color, you you would have a documentary scrapbook review of white middle class America in the heartland. And that is the takeaway: We are in our own homes; we are husbands, wives, children, and elders; we have jobs; we enjoy leisure time; we are proud folks with middle class ideals; we dress well; we have aspirations; we are black. This is 1950, mind you. Life magazine was *the* photographic news magazine. It sold more than 13 million copies a week at one point in a 40-year span in which it dominated the market. The audience was affluent America…white America.

Following *Life* magazine protocol, Parks took notes about the jobs and wages of his subjects. Most of the photos are untitled, but are accompanied by the information gathered by the photographer.

Parks met and photographed Louella Russell, the only classmate still living in Fort Scott, and her husband and teenage daughter. He roamed the town, shooting photos of friends (including a few white residents), being reminded of the strict segregation of the day as he photographed a young black couple standing under the marquee of a segregated movie theater and a baseball game at a local park. Parks recalls sitting in the "buzzard's roost" in the back upper reaches of the theater, the only place "negroes" were permitted to sit. His photo of a baseball game shows two black girls standing in what is the 'colored' section at the edge of the bleachers. As a bridge to connect with *Life* magazine's white audience, he photographed some of the white workers in town.

The whereabouts of his other classmates corresponded with The Great Migration from the South and Parks hopped on trains to look them up in Kansas City, St. Louis, and Chicago. Parks reconnected with the white residents he remembered as young boys and girls. He'd been in a fist fight on the school playground with Lyle Myrick (leaning in doorway of his father's garage) that ended up in a draw, a handshake, and a friendship. He found a disillusioned and dejected Mazel Morgan living in a Chicago tenement with her ill-tempered husband.

Did these photographs make a difference at the time? The irony is that they were not published. The photo essay and an accompanying article were slated to appear in the April 1951 issue of *Life*, but the project was discarded. The magazine's explanation is that the outbreak of the Korean War and news of President Harry Truman's firing of Douglas McArthur elbowed Parks' photos aside.

Back To Fort Scott is not a dusty relic with no relevance for us today. Americans of all races are awash daily in media coverage of racial disturbances and violence. It seems as if a police shooting of a black man or boy is photographed and videotaped nearly every week. The dense coverage tends to make us feel as polarized and segregated, riven apart, as the races in Fort Scott, Kansas in 1950. This potent little exhibition suggests that over sixty years ago some of the indispensable seeds of empathy had been sown.

Fire Fetched Down

by Jennifer Marie Donahue

When the house next door to Denise's rental caught fire, she stood outside with the other neighbors, huddled under the hood of her jacket as the rain beat down. She watched the acrid black smoke purl up from the roof as flames licked the siding and created a glowing frame around the windows on the second floor. Glass shattered, all the fragments shining as they fell away, and a stream of water gushed out in a powerful river, hitting the sidewalk and running into the street. Lightning hit it, she overheard someone say.

She realized the loud boom that had woken her from a deep sleep an hour or so before had been real. It had felt as if the walls had shook. Flashes of white light had bloomed out her window and heavy sheets of rain had drummed on the roof. Just a storm, she'd soothed herself. Yet there had been so much energy in the air, humming and conducting a kind of symphony, that her brain hadn't been able to find a quiet space for sleep after that. The ringing sirens had not been notable at first, but had blended into the sound, like the punctuation of a kettle drum or twang of a cymbal. The swirling pattern of red lights on her wall had been real.

The firefighters she watched now, masked and towering in their layers of repellant, heavy coats and pants, were real.

"They're out of town," the woman next to Denise said.

"Don't they have a cat?" Denise asked. She remembered seeing an orange tabby sunning itself in the window before.

The man standing next to the woman laced his arm into hers and shook his head.

"Maybe not anymore they don't."

No one spoke again; there was nothing left to say. There was only the responsibility to remain and bear witness.

Denise and the other neighbors stood outside for the better part of two hours, until all the fire had been extinguished and the house sat lonely and dark. Denise finally went back into her house and paced the floor as she waited for the coffee to brew. What would she save? Pictures, mementos, perhaps that small gold watch her grandfather had given her? The more she thought about it, the more she realized that she had nothing to save. She wondered if she should get a cat, despite her allergies. She could wear gloves to pet it.

The fire became a sort of touch point in her mind, an extension of those racing, persistent thoughts at night: Had she locked the front door? Checked under the bed? Turned off the oven? Left a candle burning? She never lit candles, though she had them in abundance. Her mother, every holiday and every birthday, sent her scented candles that smelled like pies, jack o'lanterns, apples, and the ocean. It was the kind of gift you could give to anybody.

Megafauna

by Erica Anzalone

My hairstylist says
she loves Las Vegas
because it's covered
in rhinestones.
I love rhinoceroses.
They are my favorite
odd-toed ungulates.
When rhinoceroses
get together
it is called a *crash*.
I would like
to get together
with others
of my kind
and call it *cash*.
Sandy nods.
Megafauna she says
can range
from large
animals to animals
that are large
compared to others
in their species
like Justin Bieber.
She taps his poster
forehead on the wall.
He had his horn removed.

He is related
to the dragonfly.
She runs the crotch
of the scissors
along the hair
at the side of my face.
The cold metal
grazes my cheek.
Have you ever heard
a lobster scream
in a pot of boiling water?
No.
Have you ever seen
a dragonfly
eat a butterfly?
No.
Marilyn Monroe's eyes google.
I throw my two cents
into the bag
bulging with kittens.
Dragonflies have multifaceted
eyes all over their head
and six legs but they can't walk well.
She grasps my head
with both hands.
She scratches my scalp
better than
one of those head
massagers you can buy
at a stall in the mall.
They look like big copper spiders,
you know?
I know.

Your Beautiful Robot Face!

by Dustin Luke Nelson

Look at your beautiful robot face!
That smile. I feel like I can see
what you'll look like when you're older.
Imagine that! You'll be an adult robot
some day. Your levers will need oiling;
your motherboard will become outdated.
Your shiny new wheels will seem silly
when they are replaced by something
that doesn't even exist yet!
The future is exciting
and full of death.
You'll be scrapped
just like I will be
and just like your mother will be
and just like your grandparents have been.

Contributors

Erica Anzalone is the author of *Samsara*, winner of the 2011 Noemi Press Poetry Award. Her poems have appeared or are forthcoming in *Denver Quarterly, Pleiades, Juked, Hotel Amerika, Mary, Sentence, The Colorado Review, The Literary Review, baldhip, Cream City Review, Pangyrus, The Offending Adam*, and elsewhere.

Carrie Bennett is the author of Washington Prize-winning *biography of water* and three chapbooks from Dancing Girl Press: *The Quiet Winter, Animals in Pretty Cages*, and *The Affair Fragments*. Her second book, *The Land Is a Painted Thing*, was selected by Kimiko Hahn for the Hilary Tham Capital Collection. She holds an MFA in poetry from the Iowa Writers' Workshop where she was a Maytag Fellow and is a Massachusetts Cultural Council Artist Fellow. She teaches writing at Boston University and lives in Somerville, Massachusetts, with her family.

David Blair is the author of *Ascension Days* (Del Sol Press, 2007) and *Arsonville*, which will be published by New Issues Poetry & Prose in 2016. He teaches at the New England Institute of Art in Brookline, Massachusetts.

Harvey Blume is an author (*Ota Benga: The Pygmy At The Zoo*, 1992), freelance writer and critic, who hails from the other Brooklyn, the part they haven't branded yet.

Kara Candito is the author of *Spectator* (University of Utah Press, 2014), winner of the Agha Shahid Ali Poetry Prize, and *Taste of Cherry* (University of Nebraska Press, 2009), winner of the Prairie Schooner Book Prize in Poetry. Her work has been published in *AGNI, The Kenyon Review, jubilat, Drunken Boat, Forklift, The Rumpus, Indiana Review*, and elsewhere. Candito is the winner of a Pushcart Prize and the recipient of scholarships and awards from the Bread Loaf Writers' Conference, the Council for Wisconsin Writers, the Vermont Studio Center, the MacDowell Colony, and the Djerassi Resident Artists Program. She is a co-curator of the Monsters of

Poetry reading series, the Editor-in-Chief of *Driftless Review*, and a creative writing professor at the University of Wisconsin, Platteville.

Claudia Cortese has two chapbooks—*Blood Medals* (Thrush Poetry Press) and *The Red Essay and Other Histories* (from Horse Less Press). Her poems and lyric essays have found homes at *Black Warrior Review, Blackbird, Crazyhorse, Kenyon Review Online,* and *Sixth Finch,* among others. Cortese lives in New Jersey and is the poetry editor for *Swarm* (swarmlit.com).

Dwight Livingstone Curtis is a writer and teacher living in Massachusetts. His fiction has appeared in various journals and magazines, including *Explosion-Proof Magazine, Yolk NY*, and *The Harvard Advocate*. He is a recipient of Harvard's Louis Begley Prize for Fiction.

Jennifer Marie Donahue was born in Virginia, but currently resides in Massachusetts. Her work has appeared at Corium Magazine, Necessary Fiction, Neon, and elsewhere. She is currently hard at work on a novel-in-stories.

Mitchell Krochmalnik Grabois has had over seven hundred of his poems and fictions appear in literary magazines in the U.S. and abroad. He has been nominated for the Pushcart Prize for work published in 2012, 2013, and 2014. His novel, *Two-Headed Dog*, based on his work as a clinical psychologist in a state hospital, is available for Kindle and Nook, or as a print edition. He lives in Denver.

Molly Howes's work has appeared in *The New York Times, Boston Globe Magazine, Bellingham Review, Tampa Review*, and elsewhere. She is a grateful recipient of fellowships from Ragdale and the MacDowell Colony and recently completed her memoir, *The Temporary Orphan: A Tale of Invisible Wounds and Unexpected Grace*. She is a sports fan.

Sebastian Johnson is the coeditor of *unfettered equality*, a blog that offers Millennial perspectives on politics, pop culture, and current events. Its editorial mission is to cultivate and explore the growing overlap in libertarian and progressive politics as an antidote to our broken political system. Sebastian is currently a fellow at the Institute on Taxation and Economic Policy, where he specializes in state tax policy. He earned a Masters in Public Policy from the Harvard Kennedy School of Government in May 2014. His areas of policy expertise are transportation, education, economics, budget and taxation, and housing. Prior to that, Sebastian taught third grade at a charter school in Lawrence, MA. He has also worked in politics at the local, state and federal level.

Judy Kugel A graduate of the University of Michigan and Boston College, Judy is the former Associate Dean of Students at Harvard's John F. Kennedy School of Government and the co-founder of the Boston Project for Careers, a nonprofit organization formed to develop opportunities for individuals seeking part-time professional positions. She is the author of numerous personal essays and travel articles in newspapers and magazines. Exploring transitions has been a theme throughout Judy's career and she has taught workshops on that subject. A determined journal writer, she has been blogging twice-weekly for seven years at www.70-something.com

Lance Larsen, poet laureate of Utah, has published four poetry collections, including *Genius Loci* (University of Tampa Press, 2013). His poems and essays appear in such venues as *Southern Review, The Times Literary Supplement, Orion, New York Review of Books, Poetry, Brevity,* and *Best American Poetry 2009.* His essays have made the Notables List in *Best American Essays* four times. He has received a number of awards, including a Pushcart Prize and a fellowship from the National Endowment for the Arts. He teaches at BYU and recently directed a study abroad program in Madrid.

Erica Lehrer is a sociocultural anthropologist and curator. She is currently Associate Professor in the departments of History and Sociology & Anthropology at Concordia University, Montreal, where she also holds a Canada Research Chair, and is the Founding Director of the Centre for Ethnographic Research and Exhibition in the Aftermath of Violence (CEREV). She is the author of *Jewish Poland Revisited: Heritage Tourism in Unquiet Places* (Indiana University Press, 2013), and coeditor of *Curating Difficult Knowledge: Violent Pasts in Public Places* (Palgrave-Macmillan, 2010), *Jewish Space in Contemporary Poland* (Indiana University Press, 2015), and *Cura-*

torial Dreams: Critics Imagine Exhibitions (McGill-Queens). In summer 2013 she curated the exhibit *Souvenir, Talisman, Toy* at the Seweryn Udziela Ethnographic Museum in Krakow, and in 2014 published the accompanying book *Lucky Jews* and the online exhibit www.luckyjews.com.

Tony Mancus is the author of a handful of chapbooks, most recently *Again(st) Membering* (Horse Less Press) and *City Country* (from Seattle Review). In 2008, he and Sommer Browning co-founded Flying Guillotine Press. They make small books. He currently works as a technical writer and lives with his wife Shannon and their two yappy cats in Arlington, VA.

Suzanne Matson is the author of three novels from W. W. Norton, most recently, *The Tree-Sitter*, and two volumes of poetry from Alice James Books. A 2012 recipient of a National Endowment for the Arts Fellowship in fiction, she is also a past recipient of a Massachusetts Cultural Council fiction writing fellowship. Her essays have appeared in *The New York Times Magazine, Harvard Review*, and other venues.

Dan Mazur is an independent cartoonist, editor, publisher and author who lives in Cambridge, Massachusetts. His comics have appeared in numerous anthologies, and his *Cold Wind* (with Jesse Lonergan), was named a notable in *The Best American Comics of 2013*. He is the co-writer with Alexander Danner of *Comics: A Global History, 1968 to the Present*. He is co-founder of the Boston Comics Roundtable, and MICE: the Massachusetts Independent Comics Expo, and founder of Ninth Art Press, a small press devoted to comics and comics anthologies, which has recently published *SubCultures: a Comics Anthology*. www.danmazurcomics.com

Kevin McLellan is the author of *Tributary* (Barrow Street, 2015), and the chapbooks *Shoes on a Wire* (Split Oak, 2015) runner-up for the 2012 Stephen Dunn Prize in Poetry, and *Round Trip* (Seven Kitchens, 2010), a collaborative series of poems with numerous women poets. He has recent or forthcoming poems in journals including: *American Letters & Commentary, Barrow Street, Colorado Review, Crazyhorse, Kenyon Review Online, Spoon River Poetry Review, Western Humanities Review, Witness*, and numerous others. Kevin lives in Cambridge, MA.

Dustin Luke Nelson is the author of the forthcoming collection in the office hours of the polar vortex (Robocup). His 90-minute performance film *STRIKE TWO* debuted with Gauss PDF in April 2014 and his performance piece *Applause* debuted at the Walker Art Center's Open Field in June. His poems have appeared or will appear in the *Greying Ghost Pamphlet Series, Fence Magazine, Paper Darts, Opium, 3:AM, The Nervous Breakdown*, and elsewhere. His digital self is housed at dustinlukenelson.com.

Janine Oshiro is the author of *Pier*, winner of the 2010 Kundiman Poetry Prize, published by Alice James Books. She has been awarded the 2013 Asian American Literary Award for Poetry and the 2011 Elliot Cades Award for Literature in Hawai'i. A graduate of Whitworth University, Portland State University, and the University of Iowa Writers' Workshop, she currently lives in Hawai'i.

Gus Rancatore was raised in New York and New Jersey and came to Boston to finish college and make ice cream. He opened Toscanini's in 1981. Gus considers toast an entry-level drug to pizza.

Shanoor Seervai is an Indian writer and journalist. Her work has appeared in *The Wall Street Journal, The Daily Beast, Guernica Magazine, The Caravan* and *The Indian Express*. Born and raised in Mumbai, she now lives in Cambridge, Massachusetts, where she is pursuing an advanced degree in public policy at the Harvard Kennedy School of Government.

Jared Yates Sexton is an Assistant Professor of Creative Writing at Georgia Southern University and currently serves as Managing Editor of the literary magazine *BULL*. His work has been nominated for a pair of Pushcarts, The Million Writers Award, and was a finalist for The New American Fiction Prize. His first book, *An End To All Things*, is available from Atticus Books.

Lisa Shannon is a human rights activist and author of *Mama Koko and the Hundred Gunmen: An Ordinary Family's Extraordinary Tale of Love, Loss, and Survival in Congo*, and *A Thousand Sisters: My Journey Into the Worst Place on Earth to Be a Woman*.

Paul A. Tamburello, Jr., a retired Brookline 4th grade teacher, lives in Watertown, MA. He dances, gallivants, and travels and writes about it here.

Whit Taylor is a cartoonist, editor, and writer from New Jersey. She received a Glyph Award and two nominations for her autobiographical comics *Watermelon* (2012) and *Boxes* (2014), as well as an Ignatz nomination for her miniseries *Madtown High* (2013). Some of her latest works include *The Anthropologists* (Sparkplug Books), which was selected as a Notable Comic for Best American Comics 2015, *Ghost* (self-published), and *SubCultures: A Comics Anthology* (editor, Ninth Art Press). Whit has also written about small press comics for *Panel Patter*, *The Comics Journal*, *The Tiny Report*, *Nat Brut*, and *Comics Workbook Magazine*.

Joelle Thomas is a graduate of the Masters in Public Policy program at Harvard's Kennedy School. She is passionate about climate change, the arts, and travel. Joelle worked on USAID projects in the Middle East and North Africa during the Arab Spring uprisings, and spent this past summer working in Paris at the International Energy Agency and having picnics on the Seine. In another life, Joelle is also an actor and singer.

Susan Volchok is a New York writer who has published widely in journals and anthologies; in mainstream magazines and newspapers, including *The New York Times*; and online in *n+1*, among other sites. *I Want To Tell You Something* is the title story from her first short fiction collection. Her website is: www.susanvolchok.com.

Michael Walsh is the author of *The Dirt Riddles* (2010), recipient of the Miller Williams Prize in Poetry from the University of Arkansas Press, as well as the 2011 Thom Gunn Award for Gay Poetry. His poetry chapbooks from Red Dragonfly Press include *Adam Walking the Garden* (2004) and *Sleepwalks* (2012). His short stories on rural queer life have appeared in *Fiction on a Stick* from Milkweed Editions and in *Fiddleblack*. He lives in Minneapolis.

Jonathan Weinert is the author of *Thirteen Small Apostrophes* (Back Pages, 2013), a chapbook, and *In the Mode of Disappearance* (Nightboat, 2008), winner of the Nightboat Poetry Prize. He is coeditor, with Kevin Prufer, of *Until Everything Is Continuous Again: American Poets on the Recent Work of W.S. Merwin* (WordFarm, 2012). Jonathan received a 2012 artist's fellowship from the Massachusetts Cultural Council. Recent poems appear or will appear in *Rattle, Plume, Unsplendid, Harvard Review, 32 Poems,* and *Copper Nickel.* He lives in Stow, Massachusetts, with the poet Amy M. Clark and their son, Jonah.

Corky White still considers herself a Minnesotan after many many decades in Boston but prefers sushi to hot-dish. Corky teaches Japanese studies and food anthropology at Boston University and thinks the best toast is Japanese.

ABOUT PANGYRUS

Pangyrus is a Boston-based group of writers, editors, and artists with a new vision for how high-quality creative work can prosper online and in print. We aim to foster a community of individuals and organizations dedicated to art, ideas, and making culture thrive.

Combining Pangaea and gyrus, the terms for the world continent and whorls of the cerebral cortex crucial to verbal association, Pangyrus is about connection.

INDEX by AUTHOR and GENRE

POETRY

Erica Anzalone	Megafauna	169
Carrie Bennett	Expedition Notes	129
David Blair	Allegheny Cemetery Day in Winter	20
Kara Candito	NOW IT IS JOY THAT IS PROHIBITED	56
Claudia Cortese	the dark, it quivers	13
	What Lucy Feels Like	33
Lance Larsen	Aphorisms for a Lonely Planet	127
Tony Mancus	That the mind isn't guided	35
Kevin McLellan	Crows with Sun	14
Dustin Luke Nelson	Your Beautiful Robot Face!	171
Janine Oshiro	Greetings from Paradise	31
Michael Walsh	Switch or Axe	71
Jonathan Weinert	The Truth of Low-Hanging Clouds	98

FICTION

Dwight Livingstone Curtis	The Pervert	100
Jennifer Marie Donahue	Fire Fetched Down	167
Mitchell K. Grabois	Astronomy	132
Suzanne Matson	Manger	36
Jared Yates Sexton	One of Those Calls	15
Susan Volchok	I Want to Tell You Something	93

ESSAYS and COMICS

Harvey Blume	Oliver Sacks: A Hero's Journey	73
Molly Howes	Boys of Summer	155
Sebastian Johnson	The War at Home: Baltimore	22
Judy Kugel	I Blog Therefore I am	147
Erica Lehrer	Lucky Jews	63
Dan Mazur	Esperantists	135
Gus Rancatore & Corky White	Toast	49
Shanoor Seervai	Reporter's Notebook: Brothels of Mumbai	89
Lisa Shannon	Congo: One Family's Endurance	58
Paul A. Tamburello, Jr.	Return to Fort Scott	163
Whit Taylor	The Synthetic Option	41
Joelle Thomas	Nous Sommes Paris	26